TROPIC OF LUST

TROPIC OF LUST

A N O N Y M O U S

Carroll & Graf Publishers, Inc.
New York

Tropic of Lust was previously published by Carroll & Graf as *Michele*.

First Carroll & Graf edition of *Tropic of Lust* 1992

Carroll & Graf Publishers, Inc.
260 Fifth Avenue
New York, NY 10001

ISBN: 0-88184-830-1

Manufactured in the United States of America

TROPIC OF LUST

CHAPTER ONE

Michele was taking the plane from London to Bangkok. All that she could perceive on her first glimpse at the inside of the plane was the odor of new leather, the thickness and the silence of the carpets, and the lighting of another world.

She couldn't understand what the smiling man who was guiding her had said, but she wasn't worried. Perhaps her heart was beating more quickly, but it was not out of apprehension or bewilderment. The blue uniforms, the signs of attentiveness, and the authority of the personnel charged with welcoming and initiating her all gave her a feeling of security and euphoria. As for the rites she had to go through at the various counters—whose mysteries she had not even tried to understand—she knew that their object was to give her access to a universe that would belong to her for twelve hours of her life: a universe with laws that were restricting but delectable. This structure of winged metal would soon be sealed and the freedom of the outside world would give way to the leisure and quietude of the flight.

They pointed out her compartment. It was uniformly covered and had no holes. The traveler could see nothing beyond that silky wall. What difference did it make? Michele wanted nothing more than to give herself up to the softness of those deep armchairs, to be numbed between their soft arms, to lean against their shoulders and on their long siren's legs.

She didn't dare stretch out yet as the steward had invited her to do, showing her the controls that made the back go down. He pressed a button and a lilliputian beam of light traced a bright ellipse over her knees.

A hostess walked by with her hands flying, placing the light honey-colored leather bag which Michele had brought over her seat in a little compartment. The hostess spoke French and the feeling of dizziness that Michele had been experiencing for two days in a foreign country went away.

The young girl leaned over her and her blondness made Michele's long hair seem even darker. They were both dressed almost identically: blue skirt, white blouse and shantung jacket. But as light as the English girl's bra was it deprived her silhouette of the mobility which Michele's naked chest disclosed. And, while the rules of the company forced the stewardess to button her blouse up to her neck, Michele's blouse was open in such a way that an attentive spectator could make out the profile of a breast either by chance or with the complicity of a sudden air current.

Michele was happy that the hostess was young and that her eyes were like her own—dark with tiny chips of gold.

Her compartment, she heard the girl say, was the last in the plane and the closest to the tail. This would insulate Michele from all the jolts that the other parts of the plane would experience (and here the young girl's voice filled with pride) ; on board this plane the comfort was not the same everywhere, because obviously the passengers in the tourist class would not benefit from as much space around them nor from such soft seats or the privacy of the velvet curtains between each row of chairs.

Michele wasn't ashamed of these privileges nor of the fortune she had to spend to procure them. On the contrary, she experienced an almost physical pleasure at the thought of the excess of attention of which she was the object.

Now the hostess was boasting about the management of the rest rooms, which she would let her passengers visit as soon as the flight had begun. There were a sufficient number on either side of the plane so that Michele wouldn't have to worry about walking a great distance. If she desired, she would only have to come in contact with the three people who were sharing her compartment. But if, on the contrary, she preferred a little company, then it would be easy for her to become acquainted with the other passengers by walking along the aisles or sitting down at the bar. Did she wish something to read?

"No," said Michele, "no thank you. You are very sweet. I don't want to read at the moment."

She wondered what she could do to please the hostess. Should she show interest in the plane? What speed were they flying at?

"Over seven hundred miles an hour with only one intermediary stop." Michele's trip would thus take no more than half a day. But, since she was going to lose time turning in the same direction as the earth, she would not arrive in Bangkok before nine o'clock the next morning, local time. Therefore, she would barely have time to have dinner, get some sleep, and get dressed.

Two children, a boy and a girl, so identical that they could only have been twins, parted the curtain. Michele noticed their conventional and ungraceful behavior, indicative of English schoolchildren, their almost Russian blondness, their expressions of affected coldness, and the arrogance with which they spoke in short phrases that they spit from their lips to the company employees. Although it seemed that they were no more than twelve or thirteen, the sureness of their gestures assured a distance between them and the employees which the stewardess would not have dreamed of attempting to breach. They placed themselves squarely in their seats which were separated from Michele by an aisle. Before she had a chance to examine them in detail, the last of the four passengers for whom the compartment had been reserved entered and the young woman's attention turned to him.

He was over a head taller than she, with a resolute chin and nose, black hair and mustache. He smiled at Michele, leaning over her a little to place a dark leather briefcase in the compartment over the seats. Michele liked his amber suit and white shirt. She thought he was elegant and well-bred which are, after all, the essential qualities that one expects from a neighboring traveler.

She tried to guess his age—forty, fifty? He must have lived well because of those little lines of indulgence around his eyes. His presence was more agreeable, she thought, than that of those pretentious little brats. But she immediately laughed at herself for this hasty aversion. It was useless—they would only be together for one night! She fell back into indifference.

Or rather, she forgot the children and the man. As she relaxed, the sensation of irritation which had been floating between the waters of her mind for a moment left her and was no longer spoiling the pleasure of her departure. The hostess, profiting by the commotion that the arrival of the new passengers had created, had left their compartment and through the gap in the curtains, Michele noticed her blue hips pressed against an invisible voyager. She hated herself for her jealousy and tried to turn her eyes away. A phrase from somewhere ran through her mind like a sad chant: "In solitude and in abandonment." She shook off the feeling, her black hair whipping her cheeks and flowing over her face. The hostess, finished with her duties for the moment, returned to the back of the plane, appearing between the draperies whose lazy legs she parted with her hands. She went over to Michele.

"Would you like me to introduce you to your traveling companions?" she asked and, without waiting for an answer, she announced the man's name.

Michele thought she heard "Eisenhower" which amused her and made her miss the twins' names.

Now the man was speaking to her. What could she say to him? The hostess saw Michele's embarrassment and questioned her compatriots, laughing and uncovering the tip of her tongue.

"What a shame," she said. "None of your companions knows any French. What a marvelous opportunity for you to refresh your English!"

Michele tried to protest, but the young girl had already turned, moving her fingers in a hermetic and gracious sign to the passengers. Then she was gone. Michele was alone. She wanted to sulk, to be disinterested in everything.

Her neighbor persevered and tried to articulate sentences whose fruitless good will made her smile. She made an apologetic expression and confessed in a childish voice: "I don't understand!" He resigned himself and was silent.

Just then a loudspeaker came on. After the English announcer had finished, Michele recognized the stewardess' voice slightly altered by the amplifier and speaking French *(for me,* she told herself). She welcomed her passengers, gave the time, the list of the crew members, notified them that the takeoff would be in a few minutes, that their seatbelts should be buckled (a steward came up to adjust Michele's himself), and that the passengers were requested not to move as long as the red light was on.

Hardly more than a murmur, a shiver of the soundproof compartments, gave away the sound of the motors being started. Michele didn't even notice that the plane was rolling along the runway. It took her a long time to realize that she was flying.

She only guessed it when the red signal went out and the man got up and offered to hang up her suit jacket which she had kept on her knees. She let him. He smiled again, opened a book and didn't look up again. A waiter appeared, carrying a tray of glasses. Michele chose a cocktail whose color she thought she recognized, but it wasn't what she had expected. It was much stronger.

* * *

What must have been an afternoon beyond the silk walls passed without Michele having time to do anything else but eat pastries, drink tea, and leaf through a magazine that the hostess had given her (she refused a second one so as not to be distracted from the novelty of flying).

A little later, they put a small table in front of her and they served her numerous dishes. A quart of champagne accompanied the meal which seemed to Michele to last for hours. But she was in no hurry as this game was beginning to please her. There were many desserts and coffee and liqueurs in immense glasses. When they came to take the table away, Michele was certain she was going to enjoy her adventure and began to savor the sweetness of life.

She felt light and a little sleepy. She noticed that she had even lost her dislike for the twins. The hostess came and went, never failing to say something nice to her in passing.

She wondered how late it was and if it was time to sleep. But in truth, wasn't she free to sleep any time she wished? Having reached that part of space in which there were no more winds or clouds, Michele could no longer even be sure whether it was day or night.

* * *

Michele's knees were naked under the gold lights. Her skirt had uncovered them and the man's eyes were now glued to them.

She was conscious that she was lifting her knees so that he could take his pleasure. But would she make herself look ridiculous by covering them? Anyway, how could she do it? She couldn't stretch her skirt any further. And why was she suddenly ashamed of her knees? She loved to have as much of her legs showing as possible below her skirts. She knew the excitement they would cause. As she contemplated the beauty of her body, she felt her temples beating more quickly and she closed her eyes. Now Michele no longer saw herself partially, but completely naked, giving in to the temptation of this narcissistic contemplation before which she knew that she would once again be defenseless.

She resisted, but only to better taste, by degrees, the delights of abandonment. This was announced by a diffuse languor, a sort of warm awareness of her whole body, a desire for relaxation and opening without any precise thoughts or identifiable emotions; nothing which was very different from the physical satisfaction that she would have experienced from stretching out in the sun on a warm beach. Then, gradually, at the same time as the surface of her lips became more brilliant, as her breasts began to swell, she stretched her legs out, attentive to the slightest contact, and her brain began to cry out images, at first almost formless but sufficient to moisten her membranes and arch her back.

Half imperceptibly, but steadily, the cushioned vibrations of the metal cocoon harmonized with Michele and blended with the rhythm of her body. A wave rose along her legs, leaving her knees, echoing inexorably on the surface of her thighs, higher and higher, making her shiver.

From then on her fantasies took flight obsessively: lips resting on her skin, male and female organs against her face, cocks touching her, rubbing against her, making a passage between her knees, forcing her legs apart, opening her cunt, penetrating her with a force that would overwhelm her. One after another they entered Michele's body, never finding an end to their voyage, traveling indefinitely inside her, taking their fill of her flesh and finally relieving themselves of their juices inside her.

The hostess thought Michele was asleep and she carefully lowered the chair, transforming it into a couch. She stretched a cashmere blanket over her long legs which the lowering of the chair had uncovered to mid-thigh. The man got up then and made the same maneuver which placed his seat next to his neighbor's. The children were asleep. The hostess said good-night and turned out the overhead lights. Only two violet nightlights prevented the objects and people from losing all form.

Michele had abandoned herself to the care the girl was taking without opening her eyes. Her dream had not lost its intensity or its urgency during the course of these movements. Her right hand was now running over her abdomen very slowly, holding back, finally reaching the level of her cunt under the light blanket which her movement was causing to undulate. But, in this darkness, who would see? With the tips of her fingers she explored herself, and crushed the supple silk of her skirt whose tightness was opposing what her legs were half-opening: they were stretching the material in their effort to part; they finally succeeded enough so that her fingers could feel through the thinness of the material the tip of erectile flesh which they sought and on which they pressed tenderly.

For several seconds, Michele let the waves subside in her body. She was trying to hold back her orgasm. But soon, no longer holding back, she began with a stifled moan to give her middle fingers the tiny and gentle impulse that would bring her orgasm. Almost immediately, the man's hand rested on hers.

Breathless, Michele felt her muscles and her nerves tense, as if a flood of icy water had been thrown at her. She remained immobile, not empty of sensations but with all sensations and all thoughts stopped in the way a film is stopped without obscuring the image. She was not afraid nor was she really restricted. She didn't have the feeling of being caught at anything either. In truth, she was not at that moment capable of formulating a judgment about the movement or the man or her own conduct. She had registered the event, then her mind had become fixed. Now, from all evidence, she was awaiting what was going to succeed her own thought.

The man's hand did not move, yet it wasn't inactive. Just by its weight it was exercising a pressure on her clitoris, on which Michele's hand was resting. Nothing else happened for a long time.

Then Michele noticed that another hand was lifting the covers and pushing them away to be able to seize one of her knees and touch it in detail. Soon it rose in a low motion along her thigh, moving over the top of her stockings.

When the hand reached her naked skin for the first time, Michele jumped and tried to escape. But, partly because she didn't know exactly what she wanted to accomplish, and partly because the man's two hands seemed too strong for her to have the least chance of escaping their grasp, she scarcely lifted her head and shoulders, brought her free hand to her abdomen as if to protect it and turned over on her side. She realized that it would have been as simple and more efficacious to press her legs together but, without being able to explain why, this movement seemed suddenly so laughable that she didn't dare do it. Finally, she renounced control over a situation that was overwhelming her, letting herself be overcome again by the paralysis that she had only succeeded in surmounting for a brief instant.

As if they intended to teach Michele a lesson for her vain revolt, the man's hands abandoned her suddenly. She didn't have time to wonder what this sudden withdrawal meant because they were on her again already, this time at waist level—sure, rapid, undoing the zipper in her skirt, pulling the material over her hips down to her knees. Then they rose again. One hand penetrated Michele's panties, which were thin and transparent like all the underwear which she usually wore—garterbelt, sometimes panties, but never a bra or girdle. In the shops where she bought her lingerie, however, she often tried on innumerable models of strapless bras, long-lines, girdles, or all-in-ones with one or another of the blonde, brunette, beautiful half-real salesgirls who would get on their knees at her feet, uncovering their long legs and moving their long, graceful fingers over her breasts or thighs and caressing her patiently with repeated, supple movements until Michele's eyes closed and she gently bent her knees, resting on the ground strewn with nylon and opened, warm, giving up to the perfect and intoxicating skill of the hands and lips.

Michele's body fell back into the position from which her show of resistance had momentarily moved her. The man caressed her flat and muscular abdomen just above the swelling of her pussy, as one strokes the neck and shoulders of a thoroughbred. His fingers ran along the folds of her groin, then above her mound, tracing the sides of the triangle. The interior angle of it was very open, a rare enough quality which Greek sculptors have nonetheless perpetuated.

When the hand that was running over Michele's abdomen had satiated itself with proportions, it forced her thighs to separate more, but her skirt around her knees was restricting their movements. They gave however, opening as much as they could. The hand caught the warm and swollen sex in its palm, caressing it as if to calm it, without haste, in a movement that followed the trail of the lips, plunging—at first lightly—between them, to pass over the erect clitoris and to come to rest on the thick pubic curls. Then, with each new passage between her legs, which were separating more and more, the man's fingers would move further, pushing more deeply between the humid moisture, slowing their progression, seeming to hesitate, as Michele's tension increased. Biting her lips to dam up the sob that was rising in her throat, arching her back, she was panting from the desire for the spasm which the man seemed to want to bring her to without ever letting her attain it.

With only one hand he was playing a rhythm and melody on her body according to his desires, disdaining her breasts and her mouth, seeming disinterested in kissing or embracing, nonchalant and distant. Michele was tossing her head from right to left and letting out a series of stifled moans, sounds which resembled a prayer. She half-opened her eyes and sought the man's face. There were tears in her eyes.

Then the hand stopped, holding on to the part of Michele's body that it had inflamed. The man leaned a little toward the passenger and took one of her hands with his other hand which he drew toward him and introduced inside his clothing. He helped her move over his rigid cock and guided her movements, regulating their amplitude and rhythm according to his desires, slowing her down or accelerating her according to the degree of his excitation, until he was sure that he could rely upon her intuition and desire.

Michele moved a little so that her arm could better serve the man and he in turn moved closer so that she could be sprinkled with the sperm that he felt forming in his glands. Yet he succeeded in holding back for a long time while Michele moved her fingers up and down, growing less and less timid, no longer restricting herself to an elementary coming-and-going motion but suddenly becoming expert, sliding along the big swollen vein, over the cock's arch, plunging as low as possible (imperceptibly scratching the skin with her long nails)—as close to his balls as the tightness of his pants permitted, then returning with lascivious torsion, until the folds in the supple skin in the hollow of her moist palm had covered the tip of the member, which she never seemed to reach as it continued to grow. Then, squeezing very hard again, the hand left for the bottom of the staff again, holding the foreskin, again and again strangling the tumescent flesh or relaxing its grip, rubbing the membrane or tormenting it, massaging with great wrist movements or with little merciless jabs. The gland, doubling its size, seemed closer to bursting at each instant. Then, at last, it came.

With a strange exaltation, Michele received the long white and odoriferous spurts which the satisfied cock finally released. It fell on her arms, her naked abdomen, her breasts, her face, her mouth, and in her hair. There seemed to be no end to it. She thought she could feel it flowing down her throat, as though she were drinking it . . . A strange pleasure came over her, a shameless ecstasy. When she let her arm fall, the man seized Michele's clitoris with the tips of his fingers and made her come.

A rumbling noise indicated that the loudspeaker was going to be used. The hostess' voice, intentionally stifled so that the passengers would not be too suddenly awakened, announced that the plane would rest at Bahrein for about twenty minutes. They would board at midnight, local time. A snack would be served at the airport.

The lights gradually came back on in the compartment, imitating the slowness of the rising sun. Michele used her blanket (which had slid to her feet) to sponge off the sperm that had covered her. She adjusted her skirt, covering her hips again. When the hostess came in, Michele, sitting up on the couch whose back she had not lifted, was still trying to fix herself up.

"Did you sleep well?" the young girl asked gaily.

Michele finished zipping up her skirt.

"My blouse is all wrinkled," she said.

She looked at the wet spots that were showing around her neck. She turned the collar out and the tip of one of her breasts appeared. The blouse remained opened like that and the eyes of the passengers were riveted to the bursting profile of the naked breast.

"Don't you have anything to change into?" asked the hostess.

"No," said Michele.

She made a face that seemed to be holding back a laugh. The two women's eyes met and recognized their complicity; their concern was the same. The man was observing them. There wasn't a single wrinkle in his suit, his shirt was as clean as at the departure, his tie wasn't changed.

"Come with me," said the hostess.

Michele got up, walked by her neighbor, and followed the young English girl into the powder room, all mirrored, with ottomans and white leather trimmings and little tables filled with lotions and other bottles.

"Wait for me!"

The hostess disappeared and came back a few minutes later, carrying a small valise. She opened it and took out a pullover that was the color of fall leaves, made of orlon, silk, and wool and so soft that you could crumple it up in your hand. When she shook it, it seemed to suddenly swell up like a rubber balloon and Michele, astounded, clapped her hands.

"You'll loan it to me?" she asked.

"No, it's a gift. I'm sure it will suit you. It's your type."

"But . . ."

The hostess placed a finger over her lips which rounded out as if to protest their embarrassment. Her tender eyes were twinkling. Michele couldn't stop looking at them. She moved toward her but the hostess had already turned around and was holding out some perfume:

"Put some of this on, it's wonderful!"

Michele washed her arms and neck and plunged the cotton pad she had impregnated with the perfume between her breasts. Then, changing her mind, she quickly undid the last buttons on her blouse.

Throwing her arms back, she lowered her silk blouse to the white carpet and took a deep breath, suddenly giddy from her half-nudity. She turned toward the hostess and looked at her with candid jubilation. The stewardess bent down to pick up the chiffon blouse. She pressed it against her face:

"Oh! It smells so good!" she cried, laughing maliciously.

Michele was losing her self-control. The incredible scene of the preceding hour seemed irrelevant at the moment. The sole thought that kept turning around in her head as if in a cage, was to get rid of her skirt and stockings, to be completely naked for this beautiful girl. Her fingers played with the zipper on her skirt.

"Your hair is so thick and black!" the hostess said ecstatically, enjoying sliding a brush through Michele's curls which fell down her naked back. It's so shiny and silky! I'd love to have such beautiful hair."

"But I love yours!" protested Michele.

Oh! if only her companion wanted to undress too! She desired it so much that her voice was hoarse. She begged:

"Can you take a bath on the plane?"

"Of course. But it would be better to wait. The bathrooms at the airport are even more comfortable. And, anyway, you wouldn't have time. We're going to land in five minutes."

Michele couldn't resign herself. Her lips were trembling. She pulled on her skirt zipper.

"Hurry up and put on my sweater," said the young English girl, holding out the woolen garment to Michele.

She helped her put her head through the tight neck. The stretch-sweater fit so well that her nipples stood out in relief as visible as if, instead of having been dressed in a sweater, they had simply been painted on. The hostess seemed to notice them for the first time.

"You're so seductive!" she exclaimed.

And she laughingly rested her index finger on one of the pointed breasts—a little like she might have pressed a doorbell. Michele's eyes sparkled.

"Is it true," she asked, "that airline stewardesses are all virgins?"

The young girl let out the laugh of a singing bird then, before Michele had time to act, she opened the door, beckoning to her passenger.

"Quick, take your seat. The red light is on. We're going to land."

But Michele looked sullen. She didn't have the least desire on top of everything to be side by side with her cabin partner again.

* * *

The landing seemed like a nuisance to her. What good would it be to know you are in the Arab desert if you couldn't see anything? The airport, aseptic and chromium-plated, strangely resembled the inside of the artificial satellite that at that very moment was showing the television programs on the screen in the waiting room where the guests were taken. Michele bathed sullenly. She drank tea, and quietly ate some sandwiches with five or six other passengers among whom were her own companions.

She looked at the man with astonishment, trying to understand what had happened between them an hour earlier. That episode didn't go with the rest of Michele's past. Was she even sure that it had really happened? Oh, how complicated it was to think about it. Too risky besides. The simplest and most prudent thing was to refuse to think about it anymore. She tried to form a vacuum in that part of her brain that persisted in posing such questions.

By the time the movement of the others, rather than the incomprehensible voice of the loudspeaker, told her that they were going to reboard the plane, she had succeeded in no longer being certain about what it was that she had taken so much trouble to forget.

* * *

When the passengers were on the plane again, they saw that it had been cleaned, put in order, and ventilated. A fresh perfume had been sprayed in the cabins. The chairs were covered with new blankets. Pillows that were shiny white and puffy made the dark blue velvet they were resting on seem even prettier. The steward came to ask if anyone wanted drinks. No? Very well! Good-night! The hostess brought her wishes for a good-night in turn. All this ceremony delighted Michele. She felt herself growing happy again—in a positive manner, with certitude. She wanted the world to be exactly what it was. Everything on earth was definitely good.

She stretched out on her back. She wasn't afraid of showing her legs this time. She wanted to move them. She lifted them one by one, bending her knees, making her thigh muscles flex, rubbing her ankles against one another with a sweet rustling of her nylons. She enjoyed the physical sensation that this exercise of her legs gave her with great pleasure. In order to be able to move better, she deliberately lifted her skirt even higher without hiding anything, pulling the material with both hands.

"After all," she thought, "it's not just my knees that deserve to be looked at, but my entire legs. You have to admit that they're really pretty. They're like two little rivers covered with dry leaves and all brimming with bad spirits which amuse themselves by jumping over one another. And that's not all I have to offer. I also love my skin that gets golden in the sun like a grain of corn but never burns; and I also love my buttocks. And also the little raspberries at the tips of my breasts with their little collars of red sugar. I would love to be able to lick them!"

The lights went out and, with a sigh of well being, she pulled the cover over her that was impregnated with a scent of pine needles which the airline company offered to protect her dreams.

When there were no lights except the night-lights, she turned on her side and tried to distinguish her cabin companion, whom she had not dared to really look at since she had again found herself stretched out next to him. To her surprise, she found the man staring at her and his eyes seemed to reach her despite the almost total darkness. They remained that way for some time with their eyes on each other in an expression of perfect tranquility. Michele recognized the sparkle of affection that was a little amused, a little protective, which she had noticed the moment they had met for the first time (when exactly? Was it only seven hours earlier?) and she thought to herself that it was this that she liked best about him.

She smiled, closing her eyes because this voyage had become so agreeable to her in such an unexpected way. She desired something vaguely—but she didn't know what. She found no other distraction than that of beginning to enjoy her beauty again: her own image danced in her head like a favorite refrain. Her heart beating, she sought in her imagination the invisible crack which she knew hid under her promontory of black herbs, at the junction of the two rivers: she felt the current coming to lick their border. When the man lifted himself on his elbow and leaned toward her, she opened her eyes and let him kiss her. The taste of lips on lips had the freshness and the saltiness of the sea about it.

She raised herself and lifted her arms in order to help him when he tried to take off her sweater. She savored the feeling of seeing her breasts jump out of the red wool which the darkness made appear even rounder and more voluptuous than during the day. To leave him the complete pleasure of undressing her, she didn't help him when he tried to find the button on her skirt. However, she lifted her hips so that he would be able to slide the zipper down without any difficulty. This time, the narrow skirt did not remain twisted around her knees: she was completely freed from it.

The man's active hands relieved her of her miniscule panties. After he had also removed her garterbelt, Michele herself rolled her stockings down and threw them down with her skirt and sweater to the foot of the couch.

Only when she was entirely undressed did he press her against him and begin to caress her from head to foot, neglecting nothing. She wanted to make love so much now that her heart was hurting her and her throat was choked—she thought she would never be able to breathe again. She was afraid, she would have liked to call out, but the man was holding her too tightly, one hand in the furrow of her buttocks, caressing the little trembling crevice, one finger completely swallowed up. At the same time, he was kissing her avidly, licking her tongue, drinking her saliva.

She moaned, little moans, without knowing exactly why she felt this pain. Was it the finger that was foraging so far into her, or the mouth that was taking nourishment from her, swallowing each breath, each sob? Was it the torment of desire or the shame of her lust? The memory of the long arched form which she had held in the palm of her hand haunted her, magnificent and stiff, hard, red, burning unbearably. She moaned so loudly that the man took pity: she finally felt his naked member, as strong as she had expected, being placed on her abdomen, and she pressed herself against him with all the softness of her body.

They held each other like this for a long moment, without moving. Then the man, seeming to suddenly make up his mind, lifted her in his arms and put her underneath him, so that she was now stretched out on the couch which was beside the aisle. Less than a few feet separated them from the English children.

She had almost completely forgotten that they existed. She suddenly realized that they were not sleeping and that they were watching her. The boy was the closest, but the girl was pushing against him to be able to see better. Immobile and holding their breaths, they were staring at Michele with their enlarged pupils from which she could read nothing but a fascinated curiosity. At the thought of being possessed before their eyes, of giving herself to this excess of debauchery, she experienced a kind of vertigo. But, at the same time, she was in a hurry to do it and for them to be able to see everything.

She was lying on her right side, her thighs and knees bent, her body offered. The man was holding her buttocks. He slid his leg between hers and introduced himself into her with an irresistible thrust which facilitated the absolute rigidity of his cock as well as the humidity of Michele's body. It was only after having reached the deepest point of her vagina and stopping for time to catch his breath that he began to move his member in large regular coming and going blows.

Michele, delivered from her anguish, panting, became moist and warm with each of the thrusts of his phallus. As if it was feeding off her, it augmented its size, its movements, and its amplitude. Through the haze of her pleasure, she succeeded in being amazed that the length of his cock could be so deep inside her. She amused herself by thinking that her organs hadn't seemed to have atrophied during so many months that they had not been stimulated by a masculine tool. This rediscovered desire made her want to profit as completely and as long as possible.

The man didn't appear close to tiring of foraging in Michele's body. She would have loved to know at a given moment how long he had been in her, but no point of respite permitted her to judge.

She held back her orgasm without it costing her either effort or frustration. She had trained herself from infancy to prolong the pleasure of waiting and she appreciated even more for the spasm to have that deep sensitivity, that extreme tension which. she knew marvelously well how to give herself.

She was used to refusing to give in to the supplication of her own body, until finally the pressure of her sensuality would carry her away, escaping in frightening tornadoes like the convulsions of the dead, but from which Michele would immediately recover more alert and cheerful.

She looked at the children. Their faces had

lost their morgue-like expressions. They had become almost human. Not exciting, not sneering, but attentive and almost respectful. She tried to imagine what was going through their minds, the confusion which the event they were witnessing must have caused them, but the thoughts died in her. Her brain was filled with stars and she was too happy to really care about the others.

When, from the acceleration of his movements, and from a certain stiffness of his hands that were grasping her buttocks and also, from a sudden swelling and pulsating in his organ, she realized that her partner was going to ejaculate, she let herself go. The flood of sperm carried her pleasure to its paroxysm. During the time he was emptying himself into her, the man held himself very deep inside her, fitting perfectly in this respect to the neck of her womb and even in the midst of her spasm Michele had enough imagination to enjoy the picture of the gland pouring out its creamy fluid—which the oblong opening of her uterus was swallowing, furtively and greedily like a hungry mouth.

The man finished his orgasm and Michele calmed down in turn, overcome by a feeling of well being that was without remorse, to which every small detail contributed: the sliding out of the male who was withdrawing, the contact of the blanket which she smelled all around her, the comfort of the couch and the warm darkness of the sleep that was coming over her.

* * *

The plane had crossed the night like a bridge, blind to the deserts of India, to the gulfs, the streams, the rice-mills. When Michele opened her eyes at dawn she couldn't see because the inside of the cabin was completely shut off from the time of day that was coloring the world outside.

The white blanket had fallen off the couch and Michele was stretched out naked on her left side, curled up like a child. Her conqueror was sleeping.

Michele regained consciousness by degrees and remained immobile. Nothing that she might have been thinking could be read on her face. At the end of a long time, she slowly stretched out her legs and turned over on her back, starting to cover herself with her hands. But her hands remained suspended: a man, standing in the aisle, was looking at her.

The stranger, in the position which he occupied with respect to her, appeared like a gigantic statue and the young woman thought that he was unbelievably handsome. It was no doubt this beauty that made her forget her nudity, or at least which didn't embarrass her. She thought: it's a Greek statue. Such a work of art couldn't be alive. A fragment of a poem came to her that was not Greek: "Deity of the temple ruins . . ." She would have liked primroses, faded herbs, in abundance at the god's feet, foliage around his pedestal, and a breeze moving the short soft hair that curled over his ears and forehead. Michele's eyes moved down the straight edge of his nose, rested on his full lips, on the marble chin. Two firm tendons sculptured the line from his neck to his shirt that was half-opened on a hairless chest. The woman's eyes pursued their study. Close to Michele's face a huge swelling was pushing out his white flannel pants.

The apparition leaned forward and took the skirt and sweater that were on the floor. It also picked up the panties and garterbelt, and the stockings and then standing up said:

"Come."

Michele sat up on the couch, placed her feet on the ground, and took the hand that was stretched out to her. Then rising with a supple effort, she moved forward, naked, as if she had changed worlds in the altitude and the night.

The stranger led her into the dressing room she had already seen with the hostess. He leaned against the silk-covered door. He placed Michele so that she was facing him. She let out a cry when she saw the Herculean reptile that was standing up in front of her out of his golden bush. Because she was much shorter than the man, the huge gland stood up right between her breasts.

The hero seized Michele by the waist and lifted her without difficulty. The young woman crossed her fingers around the masculine neck whose muscles she could feel hardening in her palms, and she separated her legs so that the scarlet member which her assailant had pushed against her could penetrate her. Tears ran down her cheeks while the man entered her carefully, tearing her despite the slowness of the assault. Michele, leaning her knees against the wall and on her partner's buttocks, helped the fabulous serpent as best she could. She writhed, scratching the neck she was clinging to, sobbing, crying out unintelligible words. She wasn't even conscious that the man was coming, and when he did it was with a thrust that was so savage that he really seemed to be trying to open a path through her right up to her heart. When he withdrew, his face calmed, he kept her standing up pressed against him. His moist phallus was refreshing to Michele's stinging skin.

"Did you like it?" he asked.

Michele placed her cheek on the Greek god's chest. She could feel his semen moving inside her.

"I love you," she murmured.

Then: "Do you want to take me again?"

He smiled. "Soon," he said. "I'll come back. Get dressed now."

He leaned over, and placed such a chaste kiss on her head that she didn't dare say anything. Before she had even realized that he was leaving her, she was alone again.

With slow movements, as if there was a ceremony involved (or because she had not completely regained consciousness), she turned on the shower, covered her body with soap, rinsed herself a minute, then rubbed her skin with warm, sweet-smelling towels. She then sprayed a perfume on her neck and chest, under her arms and on her pubic hair, which evoked the greenness of an underwood. Then she brushed her hair. Her reflection returned to her from three sides by way of the long mirrors; it seemed to her that she had never been so fresh or resplendent. Would the stranger return as he had promised?

She waited until the loudspeaker announced

the approach of Bangkok. Then, with an expression of anger, her heart on fire, she dressed, went back to the cabin, took down her bag and her coat and placed them on her knees as she sat down in the chair. Her neighbor, at whom she tossed an absentminded glance, looked surprised.

"But . . . aren't you going on to Tokyo?" he asked in English, with a shade of disappointment in his voice.

Michele guessed quite easily what he had wanted to say and shook her head negatively. The man's face fell visibly. He asked another question which she did not understand and which she didn't have the energy to answer anyway. She looked straight ahead of her with an expression of grief.

The traveler had taken out a notebook and he held it out to Michele, making a sign for her to write in it. No doubt he wanted her to leave her name or an address where he could find her. But she refused with another shake of her head. She wondered if the godlike stranger, the fantastic genie of the temple ruins would also leave the plane at Bangkok, or if he would fly on to Japan. In that case, she would see him at least on the stairs . . .

She looked for him among the passengers who, having descended the plane, were waiting under its wings to be led to the cement and glass buildings whose futuristic silhouettes stood out on the sky that was already white with heat. But she did not recognize anyone that had either his figure or his hair. The hostess smiled at her: she could hardly see her. They were already pushing her toward customs.

Someone crossed a barrier, showed a pass, and called Michele. She ran forward and, with a cry of joy, threw herself into the outstretched arms of her husband.

CHAPTER TWO

The pool in which Michele was dangling her feet was that of the Royal Bangkok Sports Club. The wives and girlfriends were admitted to this club on Saturday and Sunday afternoons to show off their legs and breasts through the thinness of their dresses, which they were allowed to display on weekdays at the swiming pool only.

Stretched out next to Michele was a lovely young woman, with the lithe, graceful body of a filly. She was speaking off-handedly to her new companion. The outcropping of muscles under her leathery skin showed up clearly in the sun like a sculptor's first draft. Her happy laugh resounded on the surface of the water. The beauty of her voice adorned her confidences.

"Donald thinks it's good form to play the injured victim since the 'Buccaneer' left. He's given me quite a time about my three night escapade. God knows how I got back to the house on the fourth after the 'Buccaneer' left!"

Michele knew that this was Diane, wife of Count de Beauchamp, Adviser to the French Embassy, and that she was twenty-six.

"Then what was troubling your husband?" asked another girl, sitting on a red chaise-longue and busily combing a blasé dog whom she called O. "Were his principles bothering him?"

"What troubled him wasn't that I spent my nights in the commander's cabin, but that I hadn't told him about it. He thought it had made him look ridiculous to be searching everywhere for me—including at the police station."

The girls went on chatting. Sprawling on the flagstone in an almost stupefied torpor, they formed a star of burning flesh around Diane who was on her stomach and Michele who was still seated. She heard them more than saw them. The warm water dancing around her legs interested her more at the moment than the spectacle of their browned bodies.

"Where did he want you to be? I suppose that's not hard to guess."

She lifted her head to question Michele. The latter could not help but admire once again the ease with which these ceramic bathers undid their bras supposedly so not to risk getting any strap marks, in reality to enlist the laws of gravity when, with an innocent appearance, they would lift themselves on their elbows to greet a friend who was passing close to them.

"My dear," proclaimed Diane, "you missed the occasion of the century, because there are only two occasions a century in Bangkok, as Barbara just remarked. A little war boat came to cast anchor in the river last weekend under the pretext of returning some favor or other to the Siamese navy. I wish you could have seen it: a crew of satyrs! The commander—dionysiac! For three whole days there were nothing but cocktails, dinners, dances—*and* the rest!"

The indiscretion, the relaxed tone, and the sharp laughs of the young French girls who were surrounding her intimidated Michele. She was surprised that the experience of a Parisian was so little help in facing this excessive society. The idleness and the luxury of these foreigners in a strange country seemed more excessive to her than anything she had ever known. Even their idleness was lived with intensity—without improvisation or relief. And everything seemed to indicate that they had only one interest—whatever their age, their appearance, or their condition—that of seducing or being seduced.

The, one with fawn-colored long hair falling profusely over her shoulders nonchalantly got up and went over to the edge of the pool where she remained standing. She then began stretching and swinging her legs, letting the clump of her sunlit young lioness' hair spread out and to Michele's suddenly attentive eyes, uncovering the moulding of her sex—a strong, well practiced sex whose impudence was exaggerated by the young girl's facial purity and graceful lines.

"David isn't so stupid," she said. "He waited for the boat to leave before bringing his wife."

"Too bad," said Diane with a sincere tone of regret. "She would have been a great success."

"But I don't see how you could think Michele would be safe in Paris," teased one of the half-naked girls. "She must not have been neglected!"

Diane looked at Michele with new interest. One of the acolytes commented calmly:

"That's true. Her husband mustn't be the jealous type leaving her all alone like that for a year."

"Not a year, six months!" Michele corrected.

She scrutinized the outline of the cunt. It was so close to her that she could have touched it with her lips by leaning over.

"I think he was right not to ask you to come here at the same time he did," interrupted O's mistress. "He spent almost all the last few months in the North; he didn't have a house yet and had to stay at the hotel every time he was in Bangkok. That wouldn't have been a life for you."

She added immediately: "How do you like your villa? I've heard that it's beautiful."

"Oh! It's hardly finished. There isn't any furniture yet. What I like especially is the garden with its big trees. You'll have to come see it," finished Michele politely.

"Won't you be alone in Bangkok three-quarters of the year anyway?" asked one of Diane's retinue.

"Why no," replied Michele, a little irritated.

"Now that the engineers are set up, David doesn't have to go to Yarn Hee: he'll have enough to do here and will spend all his time with me."

"Hah!" said the countess with a reassuring laugh. "The city is huge."

As Michele didn't seem to understand this comment, Diane explained:

"The office will take up most of his days, you'll see. You'll have all the space and leisure you want to handle your suitors. There's still a chance that the good men in this country won't be as busy as our husbands! Will you be driving yourself?"

"Yes, but I don't dare go into the labyrinth of these impossible streets. David is leaving me the chauffeur until I've learned to get around myself."

"You'll learn the essential things very quickly. And I'll guide you."

"In other words, Diane is taking on the task of corrupting you!"

"Nonsense! Michele doesn't need me for that. I'd prefer that she tell me her own pranks. Darleen is right, it's only in Paris that one can really lead a fast life."

"But I have nothing to tell," Michele objected weakly.

Suddenly she felt miserable.

"That's alright," said the girl, who seemed the most anxious to know her secrets. "You can make the most blatant confidences to us: we're like tombs!"

Silence reigned among the women for a moment. They seemed to be evaluating the significance of this declaration. Michele's sincerity had made an impression on them. The countess was looking at the new arrival with a little disgust. Was the new girl a prude? But, judging from her suit . . .

"How long have you been married?" she asked.

"Almost a year," answered Michele.

And, to make them jealous of her youth, she added:

"I was married at eighteen."

Then, for fear of letting them take the advantage again, she added:

"One year of marriage, half of which we were separated! You decide whether or not I was happy to be with David again."

To her own surprise and before she had time to turn away, her eyes filled with tears.

The young women shook their heads as if to express their sympathy. In reality they were thinking: "She doesn't belong to our camp."

* * *

"Would you like to come to the house for a milkshake?"

Michele hadn't noticed the girl who had just gotten up before. But she already liked the firm expression, the almost protective assurance of the new face—because at the same time the face was that of a little girl.

Not all that little, she corrected herself, while the adolescent was setting herself up as her guardian. About thirteen probably, but as tall as Michele. The difference was in the maturity of their bodies—there was something still awkward about the child. Perhaps it was the skin grain that linked her with childhood, a skin on which the sun's patina didn't take—which was not warm in tone, civilized, or elegant like Diane's. Michele even judged it to be a little rough at first sight . . . but not really. It was marked with tiny spots, like very fine goose-flesh, especially on her arms. Her legs seemed more shiny—beautiful boy's legs—because of the ankles with their big tendons, the knees and hard calves, and her nervous thighs. They were pleasant to see for their proportions and their strength rather than for the disturbing emotion that women's legs usually give rise to. Michele imagined these legs more easily running over the sand or stretching out on the diving-board than under the caress of a hand or opening the door of a docile body to an impatient lover.

She received the same impression from the sportive, concave abdomen, on which the scantiness of the triangular material—not more than a nude dancer ever wears—did not even seem indecent.

The little pointed tits were no more indecent even though they were poorly hidden by the symbolic strips of the bikini. "She's pretty," thought Michele, "but really, why doesn't she keep her body naked. That would be even better and I'd be quite certain that it wouldn't give anyone any naughty thoughts. She wondered what the sensuality of such young breasts could be. Then she remembered her breasts and the pleasures that she had when they still scarcely had as much shape as this young girl's, for, as she continued to look at them, they began to seem less negligible. It could be that it was the contrast with Diane's that had influenced her earlier judgment. Or else it was her narrow hips, or her youthful waist . . .

Or perhaps too it was the long thick braids that were dancing on her rosy chest. Those braids were what enchanted Michele. She had never seen such hair. So blond, so fine that it seemed almost invisible—not straw, or flax, or sand, or gold, or platinum, or silver, or ashes . . . What could you compare them to? To certain skeins of raw silk, but not completely white, that you use to embroider. Or to a sunrise. Or to the coat of a lynx . . . Michele suddenly met the green eyes and forgot all the rest.

Slanting, protracted, rising toward her temples with so rare a shape that they seemed lost on the girl's cheeks—but so green! So shiny! Michele saw, like the beams of a headlight, lights surging up and turning—lights of irony, of seriousness, of reasoning, of extraordinary authority, then, suddenly of solicitude, indeed of compassion and again, of joking malice, of fantasy, or guilelessness—the fires of enchantment.

"My name is Felicia."

And, no doubt because Michele, busy contemplating her, forgot to answer, she repeated her invitation:

"Do you want to come home with me?"

This time, Michele smiled at her and got up. She explained that she could not accept that day because David was going to get her at the club and take her visiting. She wouldn't be back until much later. But she would be so happy if Felicia came to see her the next day. Did she know where she lived?

"Yes," said Felicia briefly. "All right. See you tomorrow afternoon."

Michele profited by this diversion and left the little group. She used the excuse that she didn't want to make her husband wait. She hurried toward the clubhouse.

* * *

"Do you think the guest room will be ready in a few days?" asked Michele's husband when they sat down to lunch.

The retractable walls opened on a rectangle of water in which lotus' and morning roses were nodding their green buds.

"You can use it right now if you wish. All it needs are some curtains and multicolored cushions that I'm going to put on the bed. Oh, yes, and a lamp."

"I'd like it to be completely ready next Sunday."

"Of course, it will be. It doesn't take ten days to do that. But why do you want it finished? Is someone going to come?"

"Yes, Paul. You know . . . he has Malaria. For over a month. I invited him before you came. He just answered. Everything is working out for the best: the house itself is sending him to make a tour of Thailand. That way, he'll be able to spend several weeks with us. You'll see, he's a nice fellow. It's going to be three years since I've seen him."

"Isn't he the man who worked with you in Assoun after the construction of the dam?"

"Yes, the only one that didn't collapse."

"I remember now. You told me how serious he is . . ."

David laughed at his wife's expression.

"Serious, yes, but not completely grim! I like him very much. And I'm sure that you'll like him as well."

"How old is he?"

"Six or seven years younger than I. He was just out of Oxford at the time."

"Is he English?"

"No. I mean only half on his mother's side. His father is one of the founders of the society, but don't think that he's the same as his father. On the contrary, he's a hard worker. He's very reliable."

Michele was a little disappointed at having to share her newly rediscovered privacy with a stranger. Nevertheless, she immediately resolved to make this visitor who was so dear to her husband feel welcome. She remembered some photos in which Paul appeared as an athletic and tanned explorer, with a reassuring smile and she thought that at any rate she would prefer having him as a guest than the old pot-bellied inspectors that she would certainly have to guide through the curiosities of the city, protecting them from sunstroke and mosquitoes.

She made inquiries about other details, eager for images of the dangerous years during the time she had not known David. If he had been killed then, she never would have become his wife. This thought pulled at her heart. She couldn't finish eating.

The native boy circulated around the table, carrying coconuts filled with caramel and egg whites, after the rice pudding and the apple-fritters that the old cook with the red teeth had taken three days to prepare in honor of her new mistress. He came forward on the tips of his toes, each time looking like he was going to leap. Michele was a little afraid of him. He made too little noise, he was too strong and too supple, too well adjusted, and *always* there—too much like a cat.

* * *

Felicia arrived in a white American car driven by an Indian chauffeur with a black beard and turban. He left as soon as he had dropped her off.

"Will you be able to drive me home, Michele?" asked Felicia.

Michele was surprised by the intimacy in her voice. She also noticed more than the previous day how much the girl's voice was in harmony with her hair and her skin. She suddenly wanted to kiss the child on both cheeks, but something held her back. Perhaps it was the little pointed breasts under her blue blouse, but that was absurd! Felicia was standing very close to her.

"Don't pay any attention to what those idiots tell you," she said. "They're all braggers. They don't do a tenth of what they pretend."

"Of course!" agreed Michele after a second of incomprehension. Felicia was referring to the other women at the pool. "Would you like to go out on the terrace?"

Felicia accepted the offer by nodding her head. They went up the steps. When they passed the door to her room, Michele suddenly remembered the big nude photo of herself that David kept on his night table and she was afraid that her guest would see it. She tried to hasten her step but Felicia had stopped in front of the mosquito netting which separated the room from the landing.

"Is that your room?" she said. "Can I see it?"

She pushed the panel without waiting for an answer. Michele followed her. The visitor let out a laugh.

"What an immense bed! How many do you keep in there?"

Michele blushed.

"It's really two twin beds pushed together."

Felicia looked at the picture.

"You're beautiful," she said. "Who took it?"

Michele wanted to lie, to say it was David, but she couldn't manage it.

"An artist, a friend of my husband's."

"Do you have any other pictures? He must not have just taken this one. Do you have any where you're making love?"

Michele's head turned toward her a little. What kind of little girl was this who looked at her with her big clear eyes with such a fresh smile, posing such surprising questions in a tone of friendship without any apparent emotion. And the worst thing was that, perhaps because of this look, Michele felt that she could only tell the truth and that this child had the power to pull the most secret confessions out of her if she wanted to. She opened the door quickly as if this movement might have been able to defend her.

"Are you coming?" she asked.

Felicia smiled furtively. They went out on the terrace which was protected from the sun by a yellow and white tent. The nearby river was causing a warm breeze to blow. Felicia exclaimed:

"How lucky you are! This is the only house in Bangkok with such a wonderful location. What a marvelous view and how comfortable it is!"

She was immobile a moment before the beauty of the palms. Then, with a natural movement, she undid the belt around her waist and threw it on one of the rattan armchairs. With no further delay, she lowered the zipper of her multicolored skirt, which fell to her feet. The young girl jumped out of the circle which the material made on the floor. Her blouse came down over her hips, lower than the hem of her slip, so that all you could see of it was a narrow vertical band lined with lace. She fell back on one of the chaise-longues and grabbed a magazine, not losing a minute.

"It's been so long since I've seen a French magazine! Where do these come from?"

She stretched out with her legs side by side. Michele let out a sigh, chased away the confused thoughts that were assailing her, and stood facing Felicia. The girl burst out laughing.

"Would it bother you if I read now?"

"Why no, Felicia."

She plunged into the story. The opened magazine hid her face.

She did not remain immobile for long. Her body was already becoming alive with rapid little jumps, like the jolting of a young horse. She lifted a knee, forgetting her earlier plan, and her left thigh, that was pressed against the other, came to lean on the arm of the chair. Michele tried to steal a glance through the opening of her panties. One of Felicia's hands left the book and, without hesitation, went between her opened legs, separated the nylon and sought a point which she seemed to find and on which she concentrated for an instant. Then her hand rose, uncovering in its passage the gap between her bordered flesh. She played on the swelling that was pushing out the material, then descended again, slid under her buttocks, and began her periplus again. But this time, only the middle finger was lowered, the other fingers, lifted gracefully, framing it like opened elytrons. It caressed her skin, until her quickly bent wrist came to rest there. Michele felt her heart beating so hard that she was afraid the girl would hear it. Her tongue was pointing between her lips.

Felicia continued her game. Her finger was pressing harder, separating the flesh. Again it stopped, outlined a circle, hesitated, tapped, vibrating with an almost invisible movement. An uncontrolled sound came from Michele's throat. Felicia lowered her book and smiled at her.

"Don't you caress yourself?" she asked in a surprised voice. She leaned her head on her shoulder. "I always caress myself when I read."

Michele nodded her head, incapable of speaking. Felicia put down her magazine, arched her back, brought her hands to her hips and, in a quick movement, lowered her red panties over her thighs. She moved her legs in the air until she was free from the garment. Then she stretched out, closed her eyes and, separated the rosy membranes with two fingers.

"It's nice here," she said. "Don't you think so?"

Michele nodded again. Felicia said, in a banal, conversational tone of voice:

"I like it to take a long time. That's why I don't touch the top too much. It's better to make the coming and going motion in the hole."

Her movement illustrated her precept. Finally, her buttocks drew an arc and she let out a weak moan.

"Oh!" she said, "I can't stop myself!"

Her finger was trembling on her clitoris and the moan became a cry. Her thighs opened violently, closing again in a blow over the imprisoned hand. She cried a long time, in an almost heart-rending way, and fell back panting. Then, regaining her breath in a few seconds, she opened her eyes.

"Oh, that's so good," she mused.

And, turning her head again, she introduced her middle finger into her cunt, carefully, delicately. Michele bit her lips. When the finger had disappeared up to the end, Felicia let out a long sigh. She was glowing with health, with the satisfaction of an accomplished task.

"Caress yourself too," she encouraged.

Michele hesitated, as if in search of a means of escape. But this confusion didn't last very long. She got up quickly and opened her shorts. She slid them over her legs. She had nothing on underneath. Her orange sweater made the lustre of her black pubis stand out even more.

When Michele had stretched out again, Felicia went to sit at her feet, on a fluffy thick pillow. Now they were both in the same outfit, their breasts covered, their bellies and buttocks exposed. Felicia looked at her friend's pussy very closely.

"How do you like to caress yourself?" she asked.

"Why, like everyone!" said Michele, excited by Felicia's light breath on her thighs.

The young girl's hand, if it had been placed on her, would have delivered her from the tension in her senses and also of her embarrassment. But Felicia did not touch her.

"Show me," she said.

At least the masturbation was an immediate relief for Michele. It seemed to her that a curtain was standing between her and the world and as her fingers accomplished their familiar mission between her legs, a sense of peace grew in her. This time she did not try to prolong the waiting. She needed to find a seat again quickly, a known terrain; and she knew none better than the dazzling refuge of the orgasm.

"How did you learn to come, Michele?" asked Felicia, when her friend had recovered her senses.

"All alone. My hands discovered it themselves," said Michele, laughing.

She felt in a good mood and very talkative.

"Did you know how to do it already when you were thirteen?" asked Felicia doubtfully.

"Yes, for a long time! Not you?"

Felicia did not answer and pursued her investigation.

"And what place do you prefer to caress?"

"Oh! Several. The sensation is different at the tip or near the base. Isn't it the same thing with you?"

Felicia again paid no attention to the question. She said:

"Do you only caress your clitoris?"

"No, what an idea! The opening, you know, is much more sensitive. All I have to do is touch it with the tips of my fingers and I come immediately."

"What else do you do?"

"I like to caress myself inside the lips, where it's the wettest."

"With your fingers?"

"And with bananas (Michele's voice had an accent of pride in it)! I push them in right up to the end. I peel them first. They don't have to be that hard. The long green ones that you find hanging at the market here—they're good!"

She felt herself being aroused just by the thought of this pleasure. She was so captivated by the images of these solitary delights that she had almost forgotten the presence of the other girl. Her fingers were caressing her cunt. She would have liked something inside her at the moment. She turned over on her side, facing Felicia, closing her eyes and with her legs wide apart. She absolutely had to come again.

She rubbed the inside of the lips of her cunt with her fingers together in big, rapid, regular movements for several minutes until she was satisfied.

"You see, I can caress myself several times in succession."

"Do you do it often?"

"Yes."

"How many times a day?"

"That depends. You see in Paris I was out most of the time—at the University or shopping. I could usually only make myself come once or twice in the morning when I got up and took my bath. And then two or three times at night before going to sleep. And then during the night when I woke up. But, when I am on vacation, I have nothing else to do: I can caress myself much more. And this is going to be one long vacation!"

Then they were both silent, close to one another, savoring the friendship that was growing out of their frankness. Michele was happy to have been able to speak of these things, to have overcome her timidity. She was especially happy, without daring to admit it completely to herself, to have masturbated in front of this girl who loved to watch, who knew how to come. She had already endowed her with every capacity in her heart. And she found her so pretty now! Those elfish eyes . . . And those thighs opened without embarrassment, undisturbed by their nudity. She asked:

"What are you thinking of, Felicia? You look so serious!"

And she playfully pulled one of her braids.

"I'm thinking of bananas," said Felicia.

She wrinkled her nose and they both laughed until they were breathless.

"It's practical not to be a virgin anymore," commented the older girl. "Otherwise, no bananas! I didn't know what I was missing."

"How did you start with men?" inquired Felicia.

"It was David," said Michele, "who deflowered me."

"Didn't you have anyone else before?" asked Felicia, so obviously scandalized that Michele felt apologetic.

"No, at least not really. Naturally the boys caressed me. But they didn't know what they were doing!"

She regained her assurance and said:

"David made love to me immediately. That's why I loved him."

"Immediately?"

"Yes, the second day I knew him. The first day he came to my house. He was a friend of my parents. He looked at me all the time with an amused attitude as if he was trying to tease me. He arranged to be alone with me and asked me questions about everything: how many flirtations had I had, if I had ever made love! I was terribly embarrassed, but I couldn't stop myself from telling the truth. Just like with you! And he wanted to have all sorts of details too. The next afternoon he invited me to take a drive in his pretty car. He told me to sit down very close to him and he immediately caressed my shoulders, then my breasts, while he was driving. Finally, he stopped the car in a path in the forest and kissed me for the first time. He told me, in a tone which for some reason reassured me completely about what was going to happen: "You are a virgin. I'm going to take you." And we remained there without speaking or moving for a long time, pressed against one another. My heart finally stopped beating so hard. I was happy. This had happened exactly the way I might have dreamed it (although in reality I had never dreamed about it). David told me to take off my pants myself and I hastened to obey him because I wanted to cooperate in my defloration—not just submit passively. He had me stretch out on the car seat. He had lowered the top and I could see the green heads of the trees. He was standing in the doorway. He didn't start by caressing me. He entered me immediately in such a way that I don't remember it hurting. On the contrary, I came so well that I fainted—or fell asleep, I don't know anymore. In any case, I don't remember anything until the restaurant in the forest where we dined together. It was marvelous! David ordered a room afterward and we continued to make love until midnight. I had learned so quickly!"

"What did your parents say?"

"Oh, nothing! The next day I cried out everywhere that I was no longer a virgin and that I was in love. They seemed to find it normal."

"And did David ask you to marry him?"

"Certainly not! Neither of us had any idea of getting married. I wasn't even seventeen. I was happy just to have a lover, to be a man's mistress."

"Then why did you get married?"

"One day, David announced quite simply as

always that his society was sending him to Siam. I thought that I was going to fall down from sadness. But he didn't give me time. He continued, without any further preamble:

" 'I'm going to marry you before leaving. You'll come join me later when I have a house for you.' "

"What did you think about that?"

"It seemed too wonderful, too good to be true. I laughed like a madwoman. One month later, we were married. My parents had judged it quite natural for me to be David's mistress, but they had really screamed when he had talked about marrying me. They tried to prove that he was too old, that I was too young, 'too innocent,' even! What do you think of that? But he convinced them. I'd love to know what he told them. My father must have been tough. He couldn't resign himself to my leaving my math classes."

"What?" said Felicia.

"The year of math that I had started at the University."

"What an idea!"

Felicia burst out laughing.

"Papa's idea. David was to leave after our marriage but, by luck, he had to wait six months. Thanks to that we weren't separated immediately. I was able to be his legitimate wife as long as I had been his lover. And I found that it was as amusing to be married as it was to be a sinner. In the beginning, it seemed funny to make love at night."

"And afterward? Where did you live during his absence? With your parents?"

"Why, no! In his apartment, I mean *our*

apartment."

"Wasn't he afraid of leaving you like that, all alone?"

"Afraid? Of what?"

"Well, that you'd cheat on him!"

Michele laughed.

"I don't suppose so. We never talked about it. It probably didn't enter his mind. Mine either."

"But you did it anyway, didn't you?"

"Why, no. Some men ran after me, but I found them ridiculous . . ."

"Then, what you told the girls wasn't just a story."

"The girls?"

"Yesterday, don't you remember? You told them that you had never slept with another man other than your husband."

Michele hesitated a fraction of a second. But Felicia was too sensitive and she caught it. She turned, got on her knees, leaned on the armchair and said, suspiciously:

"There isn't a word of truth in all that. I can tell from your face."

Michele tried to lie without conviction.

"In the first place, I never said such a thing . . ."

"What! You didn't tell Diane that you never were unfaithful to your husband? That's exactly why I wanted to talk to you. Because I didn't believe you. Fortunately!"

Michele continued to protest:

"Well, you're wrong. And I repeat that I never said that the way you tell it. I simply said that I remained faithful to David all that time I was in Paris."

"And then what?"

Felicia investigated Michele's face which was set in forced unconstraint. The young girl had changed her tactics abruptly. Her voice became very sweet.

"I wonder why you would have remained faithful. There was no reason for you to deprive yourself."

"I didn't deprive myself: I didn't need anyone. It's that simple."

Felicia made a face, reflected, then questioned:

"That means that if you had wanted someone, you would have made love to him?"

"Why, yes."

"What does that prove?" said Felicia, her voice sharp, like a squabbling child.

Michele looked at her with an indecisive expression then, suddenly, she said:

"I did!"

Felicia looked like she had been electrified. She got up in a leap, sat down again, crisscrossed her legs, and placed her hands on her knees.

"You see," she moralized with a wounded expression, "you were trying to make me believe you hadn't!"

"I didn't do it in Paris," explained Michele, patiently. "On the plane. The plane that brought me here. You understand?"

"With whom?" pressed Felicia.

Michele took her time, then revealed:

"With two men whose names I don't even know."

If she had thought she was going to cause

a sensation, she failed, because Felicia didn't budge. She pursued her interrogation.

"Did they come in you?"

"Yes."

"Were they very deep inside you?"

"Oh, yes!"

Michele instinctively put her hand on her abdomen.

"Caress yourself while you're telling me," ordered Felicia.

But Michele shook her head, no. She suddenly seemed struck with aphasia. Felicia examined her with a critical eye.

"Go on, talk!"

Michele obeyed, at first reluctantly, but soon, excited by her own story, without having to be begged anymore, she forced herself not to leave out a single detail. She stopped after telling how the Greek statue had delighted her. Felicia had listened with a studious expression, changing positions several times . . . she didn't seem particularly impressed, however.

"Did you tell David?" she asked.

"No."

"Have you seen those two men since then?"

"Obviously not!"

It seemed that, for the moment, Felicia had nothing further to ask.

Michele called a little servant girl who had black flowing hair, an ochre body and wore a bright sarong and asked her to bring tea. She put her shorts back on and Felicia put her panties on. The multicolored skirt remained on the ground. The young girl then demanded to see all the photos of Michele naked and Michele went to get them. Felicia became sharp again.

"Listen. You're not going to tell me that you didn't do anything with the photographer, are you?"

"For the last time," cried Michele, "he didn't even touch me!"

And she added, pretending to be disappointed:

"Anyway, I didn't have a chance since he was a fag."

Felicia made a face. She remained skeptical. She studied the photos again.

"I think an artist should always make love to his model before doing her portrait. That was an absurd idea to go to someone who didn't like women."

"I didn't choose him," said Michele, who was beginning to get angry. "He offered to photograph me himself. I told you, he's a friend of David's."

Felicia made a gesture as if to sweep the past away.

"You really should have yourself painted by someone good. It'll be too late when you're old."

The image of what Felicia must have meant by "someone good" and that of the imminence of her own decrepitude made Michele burst out laughing.

"I don't like posing. Even for a photo. And especially not for a painting!"

"And since you've been here, you haven't done anything with men?"

"Are you mad?" said Michele indignantly.

Felicia seemed pensive, almost discouraged.

"But some time or another you'll have to find a lover," she sighed.

"Is it really indispensable?" said Michele, rather amused.

But the young girl didn't seem in a mood for joking. She shrugged her shoulders.

"You're funny, Michele," she said. Then, after a silence: "But you don't intend to continue living like an old woman, do you?"

And, this time seized by a kind of anger, she repeated:

"You're really funny!"

"But," pleaded Michele timidly, "I'm not an old woman. I have a husband!"

This time Felicia answered with a cold expression. According to every indication, the argument was distressing her. She seemed resolved not to discuss it any further. But it was Michele who now had no desire to change the subject of conversation. She tried to recreate the atmosphere:

"Don't you want to take your pants off, Felicia?"

Felicia shook her head.

"No, I have to leave (she got up). Will you drive me home?"

"Are you in such a hurry?" asked Michele, alarmed.

But she already understood that Felicia's decisions were final.

In the car the young girl stared at her in a very preoccupied way.

"You know," she said, "I don't want you to die, you're too pretty. But it's completely stupid for you to be as prudish as you are."

Michele burst out laughing. But Felicia continued quickly:

"It's unbelievable that you were able to reach your age with nothing besides your little adventures on the plane. You have really been a dolt." She shook her head sadly. "I assure you, you're not normal."

"Felicia . . ."

"Oh, no! You can't lament about what's passed."

The green light was emitting a radiance of sovereignty.

"From now on, will you at least do what I tell you?"

"What exactly?"

"*Everything* I tell you."

"But . . ."

"Swear it!"

"Oh, all right, if it will amuse you."

She continued laughing, but Felicia didn't allow herself to join in.

"Do you want me to advise you?"

"No, thanks!"

The elfish eyes analyzed the gravity of her case. Michele pretended to be involved, without any illusions about her chances of coping with Felicia. When the car stopped in front of the bank which her father managed, she said:

"Tonight, exactly at midnight, caress yourself again. I'll do it at the same time."

Michele batted her eyes as a sign of complicity. She leaned over to blow a kiss to the young girl. Felicia cried out from the distance:

"Don't forget!"

It was only after she left that Michele realized that she hadn't been able to ask Felicia the tiniest question. If the little girl with braids was going to know the intimate life of her new friend from now on, Michele, on the other hand, would be completely in the dark about hers. She had even forgotten to ask her if she was a virgin.

* * *

That night, when her husband had taken his shower and came in the room, he found Michele waiting for him, sitting on her heels completely naked on the edge of the big bed. She put her arms around his hips and took his cock in her mouth. As soon as she had sucked it several seconds, the stem began to swell and stand up. Michele moved it between her lips until it was very hard. Then she licked it up and down, pressing the bluish vein which ran on the surface and whose congestion and size augmented under her embrace. David told her that she looked like she was gnawing on a husk of corn and she bit it with her little teeth to complete the resemblance. Quickly she made up for it by gently sucking the satiny skin of his testicles. She lifted them in her hands, slid the tip of her tongue under them, caressed another vein, stuffed herself with warm blood which she felt beating harder at the touch of her lips, explored more and more intimately, going, coming, rising suddenly to the tip of the phallus, pushing it deep into her throat, so far that she was almost strangling. Then, without pulling it out, she sucked it in a slow, irresistible movement while her tongue enveloped and caressed it.

Her arms embraced her husband's hips with a passion that increased as she sucked his cock more regularly and as the excitation of her lips and tongue were communicated to her breasts and cunt. She felt a liquid as abundant as the saliva with which she was at that very moment moistening the warm apoplectic member flowing between her thighs. In order to be able to moan from desire and to let a partial orgasm soothe her and to permit her to pursue her caresses, she let go of the penis for a moment, without, however, ceasing to caress the half-opened duct with little blows from her tongue. Then she swallowed the palpitating tip of flesh again.

David had taken his wife's head in his hands, but not to guide her movements or to regulate her rhythm. He knew that he would be better off trusting her and letting her refine their common pleasure according to her desires. The style which she gave to this way of making love again distinguished her from all the others. Some days, Michele liked to play with her husband until he was ready to die. She wouldn't stay on any particular part, jumping from one sensitive place to another, pulling moans from her victim's throat, prayers to which she paid no heed, making him jump, pant, pushing him to delirium, until the moment when, with final precise gestures, she would perfect her work. But today she wanted to be the dispenser of a more serene pleasure. Without holding the vibrating cock too tightly, she added the pressure of her fingers and the regular movement of her hand to the suction of her lips—applied to relieve the organ of its semen, to empty it as much as possible. When David came, she swallowed the savory substance which she had succeeded in pulling from him in very slow gulps. But she left the final spurt, letting it fall on her amorous tongue.

She had involved herself so much in his orgasm that it was enough for her husband to press her clitoris between the lips for her to finish coming.

"I'll take you later," he said.

"No, no! I want to drink you again! Promise! Promise me that you'll come in my mouth again. Oh! you'll flow into my mouth again, tell me, tell me, if you like it! It's so good! I love it so much!"

"Did your girl friends caress you as well as I do when I wasn't here?" she asked him later when they were resting.

"What do you expect? You know there isn't a woman alive who can be compared with you."

"Even the Siamese girls?"

"Even they."

"Aren't you just saying that to please me?"

"You know I'm not. If you weren't the best of lovers, I would tell you—to help you become the best. But really I don't see what more you could learn. There must be a limit to the art of lovemaking."

Michele seemed thoughtful.

"I don't know."

She closed her eyes. The sound of her voice testified to the fact that her doubt was not feigned.

"In any case, I'm still far from an expert!" David protested.

"What makes you think that?"

She didn't answer. He insisted:

"Don't you think I'm a good judge?"

"Oh, yes!"

"Then, not a good professor? It sounds as if you're suddenly dissatisfied with your amorous education."

She hastened to reassure him.

"Darling, no one in the world could teach me better than you. But it's difficult to explain . . . I have the impression that there must be something more important in love, something more intelligent than simply knowing what to do."

"You mean the sympathy, the tenderness, the devotion?"

"No, no! It's something important. I'm completely certain that has reference to physical love. But it doesn't mean that it's a matter of supplementary relationships, or of more skill, or of more ardor. Perhaps it's a state of mind instead."

She stopped to take a breath: "I don't think it's a question of limitation. What if, on the contrary, it were a question of the angle, the manner of looking at it?"

"A different way of envisaging love?"

"Not only love. Everything!"

"Can't you explain yourself more clearly?"

She bit her lips pitifully, rolling the curls in his pubic hair around her long polished nails as if it would help her meditate.

"No," she concluded. "It's not clear in my head. There is certainly a development I must reach, something to find, which I still lack to be a true woman. But I don't know what!"

She was disconsolate—"I thought I knew so many things, but what are they next to what I don't know?"

She frowned impatiently:

"What I need first is to become more intelligent. You see, I don't know anything, I'm too innocent. I'm too much a virgin. It's terrible how I can feel so virginal tonight! Virgin everywhere, bristling with it, to the point of being ashamed of it."

"My pure angel!"

"Oh, no! Not pure! Not at all pure. A virgin is not necessarily pure. But she is ignorant."

He kissed her, enchanted with her. She persisted: "You're prejudiced!"

"It's so wonderful to hear you complaining of your innocence when I've just been delighted by your chaste lips!"

She laughed at herself, but was she convinced?

"Oh, if only it were through there that intelligence were to come to girls," she said with a great sigh, "I wouldn't let a minute more pass without pulling it out of you."

The evocation produced an effect on David that Michele soon discovered. She already was trying to put her promise into execution. She got up and darted her tongue between her moist lips . . . but he held her back.

"Who told you that it's only through that mouth of yours that intelligence enters? Remember, it blows where it wishes."

He lay down on her and she immediately desired to be taken as much as he desired to take her. She opened her cunt herself with the tips of her fingers. She guided the gland, helped him plunge inside her. She lifted her knees, surrounding the masculine body, while the hard organ pushed into her abdomen as it had into her throat earlier. For Michele, who wanted to feel it in her mouth at the same time, the exuberance of her imagination took the place of the actual act and her lips felt as though they were tasting the sweetness of the sperm. She dreamed that she was drinking his semen and the pleasure in her abdomen filled her throat. She implored:

"Come in me!"

She felt that the orifice of her womb was being probed by the phallus and swallowing it like a sucker. She wanted David to ejaculate. She tried with all the persuasion of her abdomen and buttocks to pull his liqueur from him. Every muscle of her body concurred to make an elastic and agile animal out of her who clung to the man and made him tremble with pleasure. But David wanted to conquer her, to make *her* come first. He pierced her with rapid, violent blows, with all the length and breadth of his cock, without control, his teeth clenched, eager to hear her moan. Suddenly she was scratching his back and crying so loud, so long, that the voice and breath went out of her and she calmed down and suddenly grew still, dazed, subdued, serene, scarcely aware of her body but already desirous that the excitement be born in her mind again.

For the moment she wanted him to be still. He knew it and held her, immobile. She murmured:

"I would like to fall asleep like this, with you inside me."

He placed his cheek against hers. The flood of her hair caressed his lips. They remained like that for a long time. Then he heard her whisper in his ear:

"Am I dead?"

"No, I am giving you life."

He pressed her to him and she trembled.

"Oh, my love, it's true that we are one. I am only a small piece of you."

She placed her lips on his, kissed him with all the strength and tenderness of her mouth.

"Take me again! Deeper! Open me. Tear me apart! Come in my heart! Deflower me! Oh, I love you! Deflower me!"

He joined the game:

"Give yourself more. Give in. Be complaisant. Lend yourself to what I want."

She murmured: "Yes!" She was intoxicated with submission.

"Yes," she repeated. "Do everything you want. Don't ask me: do it!"

She wanted to be able to deliver herself even more, to be even more aware of being taken according to the desires of the man who was taking her. To be at his disposition, not to be consulted, to be weak, to be yielding, to do nothing else but obey actively and openly . . . Could there be a greater happiness than to consent, she thought in secret. This thought was enough to finish making her swing into an orgasm.

Then she found herself an exhausted animal with a broken backbone, dead legs, consumed destiny—a happy trophy in the appeased shadow of the hunter.

"Do you think that I'm the woman you want?" she said.

He answered by kissing her.

"But I want to become even more so!"

"You are—more every day."

"Are you sure?"

He smiled confidently. She stopped worrying. A nocturnal current was circulating in her veins, dulling her, closing her lips. She tried to stop fighting the pleasure that was confusing her mind.

"It must be Felicia who was worrying me," she heard herself say. It surprised her, because that wasn't what she wanted to confide to David.

He was also surprised. "Why Felicia?"

"She is strangely perceptive." Michele didn't want to talk. Felicia suddenly took on the likeness of a plant that was continuing to grow in her with its insinuating roots, its infinite branches, its sap, an urgent and powerful force within her. But her husband insisted, while he slowly began to move in her and to prepare to give her his substance.

"You think she is going to reveal the secrets of life to you?"

"Why not?"

The idea amused David. "Have you already had a taste of her talents?"

She hesitated a little, and wound up lying, without caring whether he believed her or not, too occupied in another world: "No."

Then she smiled at an image—which was not

unbecoming—on the shores where her dream was landing . . .

"But I would like it!"

David sounded indulgent:

"I see," he said. He rocked her gently in his arms. "My little virgin wants to make love with Felicia, doesn't she? Is that what is tormenting you?"

Michele shook her head methodically with the exaggeration that one puts into his gestures and words when he is trying to make himself understood without having to open his eyes.

"It's not only that, but it's certainly that too," she agreed.

He made fun of her gently:

"With that little girl!"

But she had the expression of a spoiled child and her voice protested from afar, softened, withdrawn, as if in the crest of a wave:

"I have the right to want to, don't I?"

David came in her, marveling at having so much to give her, at piercing her so deeply and coming so often.

They remained stretched out side by side, touching shoulders and hips. She did not move so that not a single drop would flow out of her.

"Sleep," said David.

"Wait . . ."

In a distant room, the regular notes of a soft chime. Slowly, Michele's hand descended toward her abdomen, and her fingers touched her clitoris, penetrating her cunt that was brimming with sperm. Felicia's thighs opened before Michele's closed eyes while she responded to each movement that she saw in her dream by an identical caress. When she knew that her friend was going to come, she cried, even harder than she had cried in her husband's arms. He lifted himself on his elbow and smiled at seeing her come, naked and luminous with pleasure, one hand the captive of her abdomen, the other pressing her breasts one after another, and her legs still shaking long after her forehead, her eyelids, and her lips had been changed into the immobile sweetness of sleep.

CHAPTER THREE

Michele wanted to go to the club to swim, not to listen to gossip. Therefore she decided to go in the mornings. She swam the length of the pool ten times without caring how long it took or about the rare men who were present at that hour. The repeated movement of her arms over her head had made her breasts pop out of her strapless bathing suit. When she rolled over on her side, the water would make her skin shine. A fine circular trench would be dug around her nipples. The edges of the areola would appear to be lifted for this reason, outlining an atoll. Without this detail which recalled the vulnerability of their pulp and brought to mind their juicy taste, their curvature might perhaps have been too perfect to excite anyone. They would have been too much like the breasts on a statue.

When, panting after this exercise, Michele seized the chrome handles on the ladder, she saw that her path was being guarded. Diane was leaning over her, standing on the edge of the pool, laughing loudly.

"Road block!" she exclaimed. "Show your pass!"

Michele was disappointed that one of the "idiots" had found her. However she smiled as best she could.

"So, you're playing mermaid at an hour when good women are going shopping. What's all the secrecy about?"

"But you're here yourself," observed Michele. She tried to climb up.

Diane didn't hurry to let her pass.

"Oh with me it's not the same thing," she said, affecting an air of mystery. But Michele didn't ask her to explain.

The countess quietly surveyed her prisoner's charms.

"You're built divinely!" she admired.

She had spoken with conviction and Michele thought that she didn't seem to be teasing. Perhaps she was a little nuts, but you had to admit that she was charming. Michele didn't have to force herself to be friendly so much anymore.

Diane finally stepped away from the ladder. The swimmer pulled herself up. Deliberately she replaced her breasts into her bathing suit with her fingertips, or, more exactly, the lower half of her breasts (almost all of tne nipples remained visible) and sat down next to Diane. Two tall nordic boys came over and began a conversation in English. The countess responded cheerfully. Michele was not afraid about understanding little of what they said. Diane turned toward her suddenly and asked:

"Do these two do anything for you?"

Michele made a face and Diane undertook to advise the candidates of the failure of their campaigns. They laughed out loud, apparently without spite. But they didn't seem eager to go away. Michele found them incredibly simple. Finally her companion got up with determination and pulled on her arm.

"They're boring us," she declared. "Come on the diving board with me."

The two girls climbed the steps and lay down side by side on their stomachs on the platform. Diane quickly removed her bra and panties.

"You can lie here naked," she informed Michele. "You have time to see anyone coming from here."

But at the moment, Michele didn't want to be naked in front of Diane. She made up an unconvincing excuse: that her tight suit wasn't easy to take off and put on again; that the sun was too strong . . .

"You're right," admitted Diane. "It'll be better to get used to it gradually."

After that they let themselves be overcome by a half lethargic state. Michele found that the countess had some good points after all. She liked people with whom she could stay without talking. However it was she who broke the silence after a little while.

"What is there to do here, outside of swimming, cocktails, and dinner at Pierre's or Paul's? Don't you die of boredom?"

Diane sighed as if faced with the enormity of it all.

"Oh, it's not pastimes that we lack. I'm not talking about the movies, or the nightclubs either. You can go horseback riding, play golf, tennis, squash, water-ski on the river, or go canoeing. And why not visit the pagodas? There are over a thousand. If you see one a day, you can occupy yourself for months. It's too bad that the sea—I mean the real sea where you can swim—is so far away. But it's worth the trip. The beaches are extraordinary, long and endlessly large, bordered by palm trees, deserts, and covered with shells. The water is fabulously phosphorescent at night and crammed with thousands of little things. The corals tickle your feet, and the sharks come to eat out of your hand."

"I'd like to see that!" exclaimed Michele.

"They'll even sing you serenades if you make love in their territory—during the day under the sun with the sand or under the shade of the trees. You'll always find a little boy ready to fan you for a small fee while your gallant knight is paying his respects. And when you're lying on the sand at night with your back caressed by their tongues and your eyes protected from the stars by an amorous face, oh, then you appreciate your luck at being a woman!"

"If I understand you, that's still the favorite sport in this country?" asked Michele.

Diane looked at her with an enigmatic smile and only answered after a few minutes.

"Tell me, my dear . . ."

She stopped, appearing to calculate some mysterious probability. Michele turned toward her and laughed:

"What do you want me to tell you?"

Diane reflected in silence, then suddenly determined the confidence which the new arrival deserved. Her voice lost its tone of wordly persiflage that she had affected until then. She gave her neighbor a friendly smile.

"I'm sure," she said, "that you aren't the little hypocrite that you pretend to be. That's fortunate. To tell you the truth, you interested me immediately."

Michele didn't know what to think of this declaration. She remained on the defensive, despite herself, more angry than flattered, because she didn't like her openness to be doubted. And had those girls always judged her to be a prude? This had made her laugh at first but now was beginning to irritate her.

"Don't you want to enjoy yourself here?" pursued Diane in a tone that said more than her words.

"Yes," said Michele. She was conscious that she was travelling a dangerous road but she was more afraid of being suspected of virtue.

Diane's smile only half-rewarded her.

"Then come with me one evening. You can tell your husband that you are having dinner with the girls. Wait and see what I have in store for you! There aren't any more gallant and strong lovers than Diane's knights within fifty light-years from here. They are full of passion, young, handsome, and skillful lovers. You have nothing to fear. All right?"

"But," said Michele evasively, "you scarcely know me. Aren't you . . ."

Diane shrugged her shoulders.

"I know you enough! I don't have to observe you for long to see that you're beautiful to both men and women. And the ones I'm talking about appreciate beauty. I wouldn't have thought of introducing you if I wasn't sure of them and of you."

"And . . ." questioned Michele with hesitation. "Your husband?"

Diane laughed sincerely:

"A good husband likes his wife to be happy," she said.

"I don't know if David will find this so normal."

"Then don't confide in him," concluded Diane good-naturedly.

Then she sprang toward Michele, put her arms around her waist, and drew her to her:

"Will you swear to tell me the truth?"

Michele fluttered her eyelashes without committing herself too much. The solid, warm breasts against her shoulder made her lose her footing a little.

"You're not going to try to make me believe that you have never accepted others beside your husband in that exciting body, are you? Good. Very well, have you told him about it every time?"

Michele was on the rack again. Now the quest for confessions began! But what good would it do to defend herself? And should she pass for more innocent than she was? She shook her head negatively to Diane's question. Diane kissed her gaily on the ear.

"You see," she triumphed. She contemplated her proudly. "I promise that you won't regret having come to Bangkok!"

The tone seemed to indicate that Michele had agreed to sign a pact. She tried to escape:

"No, listen! This troubles me."

She grew bolder and said: "Don't think that this is out of prudishness or for moral reasons. It's not that. But . . . let me have some time at least to get used to the idea. Gradually."

"Of course," said Diane. "No hurry. Like the sun . . ." She seemed seized by a sudden inspiration, let her lips outline a furtive smile, and sat up.

"Come on," she said. "We'll go get a massage." She put on her bikini, then, with a little disdain in the tone she might have used on a baby, added:

"Don't be afraid, honey, there are only women there."

Michele left her car at the club and accompanied Diane in her uncovered cab. They drove for half an hour through the motor bikes and taxis that were smoking up the streets crowded with Chinese signs. They stopped in front of a new building on a single floor that was flanked by silk merchants, restaurants, and travel agencies. An inscription in characters unknown to Michele adorned the front. They pushed a thick glass door and found themselves in the reception hall of a bathing establishment, very similar in appearance to those in Europe. A Japanese girl in a flowered kimono greeted them politely, bowing several times to them with her hands crossed over her chest. Then she led them along corridors that smelled of steam and cologne. She stopped in front of a door, then bent in half again. Michele wondered if she was mute.

"You can go in here," said Diane. "All the

masseuses are good. I'll take the cabin next door. We'll meet again in an hour," she added.

Michele hadn't expected Diane to leave her alone. She felt a little helpless. The door which the Japanese girl had half-opened led to a small, clean bathroom with a very low ceiling in which a young Asiatic girl in a white nurse's smock was standing between a massage table and a bathtub. She was very tiny and had the face of a bird that had returned from many voyages. She also bowed, and said several words, without appearing to attach importance to whether she was understood or not. She then moved toward Michele and, with an attentive finger, began to undo her blouse.

When Michele was undressed, the girl motioned for her to enter the bath that was filled with a bluish, warm, and sweet smelling water. She passed a moist cloth over her client's face, then methodically soaped her shoulders, her back, her chest, and her abdomen. Michele shivered when the soapy sponge circulated between her legs.

When she had finished bathing her and had dried her in a huge warm towel, the Siamese girl invited Michele to stretch out on the table. First she beat her with the edge of her hand with little hurried blows, then she pinched her muscles, pressed on her calves and buttocks, pulled on the bones in her toes, massaged her neck for a long time, and tapped her head. Half asleep, Michele felt relaxed and happy despite everything.

The masseuse then took two objects in the shape of a pack of cigarettes out of a drawer which she placed in her hands and which immediately emitted a humming noise. Her vibrating palms slowly crept over the surface of Michele's naked body, forcing their way into every cavity or fold, sliding in the crux of her neck, under her arms, between her breasts, between her buttocks, each time with irresistible competence. Then they sought the most receptive points on the inside surface of her thighs. Michele was trembling all over. She separated her legs and lifted her pussy a little, offering herself with a movement of inimitable grace which held out the lips of her cunt as if for a child's kiss. But the hands moved away and rose toward her breasts, coming and going regularly, passing over their traces in imitation of an iron sliding over a sheet. When Michele began to moan, in a scarcely audible voice, the hands moved to her breasts, turned over them, now caressing their summit, now leaning on the nipples and making them reach the thickness of the breasts. Waves ran through Michele down to her legs. She arched herself and cried painfully for a long time. The hands continued their work on the sensitive tips of her chest until her orgasm diminished, calmed her, left her inert and soft.

Without losing any time, the masseuse brought her attention to her shoulders, her arms, her ankles. Michele slowly came to herself. She finally opened her eyes and smiled. The young Siamese girl returned it with a formal attitude, then asked what had the sound of a question. At the same time, she brought her long fingers toward Michele's abdomen, looking at her with her eyebrows raised as if awaiting permission. Michele nodded her head "yes." The hand, weighed down by the vibrator, executed the movements on the surface and in the folds of her cunt, knowing exactly what was needed at each instant to give the most pleasure. She did not take any precaution to be gentle, nor did she take any respite, certain of the result, adding the virtuosity of her palpitations to the power of the electrical vibrations.

Michele held herself back with all her strength, but her resistance was of short duration. She came again, so violently that even the masseuse looked a little frightened. A long time after the hands had withdrawn, Michele continued to writhe, shaking, gripping the edges of the white table.

"The walls have been soundproofed," said Diane when they met at the door. "Now you're not going to tell me that you prefer mathematics."

* * *

Felicia returned to Michele's house four successive afternoons. Each time, she made her undergo a more demanding interrogation, including precise details about her relationship with her husband as well as the incontinence of her daily dreams.

"If you had really given yourself to all the men you did in in your imagination," she observed one day, "you'd be an accomplished woman."

"You mean that I'd be dead," replied Michele, laughing.

"What do you mean?"

"Do you think you can make love with men as often as you can by yourself?"

"Why not?"

"Because it's tiring to be taken by a man!"

"And doesn't it ever tire you to caress yourself?"

"No."

"How many times do you do it now?"

Michele smiled modestly.

"Yesterday I did it a lot, you know. I think it was at least fifteen times."

"There are women who do it that much with men."

Michele shook her head. "Yes, I know." But she didn't seem tempted.

"You see," she argued, "it's not always so exciting with men. They're heavy and it even hurts sometimes. And that's not really the way girls like to come the best . . ."

Paradoxically, there was only one kind of confidence that Michele did not dare openly make to the young girl. From time to time she made allusion to it without succeeding in guessing whether Felicia understood or not. She herself couldn't explain a timidity and a discretion which nothing in her visitor's conduct seemed able to justify. As soon as she arrived, Felicia undressed. She hadn't even argued when Michele had suggested she take off her slip and the two girls passed their meeting completely naked from then on, on the terrace, surrounded by trees. Nevertheless, the emotion that Michele felt showed only in the multiplication of the caresses she practiced on herself. She didn't dare touch her friend or invite her to touch her, although she desired it to the point of losing sleep over it. A strange modesty and a strange immodesty were arguing in her heart.

She came to wonder—confusedly and refusing to really reflect upon it deeply—whether this unprecedented reserve was not in reality a superior refinement newly invented without her knowledge by the intuition of her senses and whether the deprivation of Felicia's body which she inflicted upon herself against all instinct and all reason, did not ultimately have a more subtle taste, a more perverse attraction than a physical relationship. Thus Michele discovered in this situation that would normally have made her suffer—in which a little girl disposed of her according to her whim without conceding anything to her partner's tastes in return—an unexpected source of sensual delight.

In the same way that a strange passion surged from the frustration of a woman to whom all carnal desires had always seemed terribly natural and to which she had attached the greatest importance, another erotic value was revealed to her because of the remarkable secrecy which her little friend kept about her own sexual life. While Michele was aware of the ease with which she resigned herself to knowing nothing—or almost nothing—about Felicia, she realized that the girl experienced more physical and intellectual pleasure in offering to another individual the spectacle of her lust than she would not have had as a spectator. And, if Michele was impatient to see her friend every day, it was less for the excitement of seeing her naked or witnessing her lascivious games, than it was infinitely more scandalous and, consequently, more delicious, to caress herself, stretched out on her chaise longue, under Felicia's attentive eyes. When the young girl left, the charm wasn't broken: Michele still imagined the green eyes staring at her cunt and she would continue to masturbate until evening.

* * *

The Wednesday which followed their first meeting, Michele was invited to tea at Felicia's mother's house. She found about ten "ladies" in the pretentiously furnished parlor. All of the women appeared perfectly insignificant to her. She was already regretting not being able to be alone with her confidante whom she saw sitting on the floor performing her duties as a model little girl, when her interest was suddenly reanimated by the arrival of a young, very elegant woman, at first sight as displaced in this assembly as she was herself.

The new guest made Michele think of the Parisian models she had loved. She had their slender build, the imponderable lassitude, and the illusory distance. Her mouth was half-opened, her huge eyes were framed by amber eyelashes, and the sweet curve of her eyebrows modeled so improbable an innocence over her face that it did not seem real. Michele thought tolerantly that she was no doubt the only one in this room who, by what she called her "experience" could understand how much passion could be hidden behind the detachment of the girl's stony gaze. This reflection was charged with an ambiguous emotion for Michele. Equally involved were the still recent savor of her schoolgirl excitement and the more adult passion she had experienced in Paris dressing rooms. She thought that she herself would like to become a work of art, that arriving in Bangkok like clay, it would be good for her to find form there (she was thinking less of the form of her body—which she had no reason to wish to change—than of that of her mind). And, although she didn't picture exactly what this accomplishment would consist of, she wished that her life would one day become something precious and successful like the complicated style of this girl's bronze hair, triumphant like those grey eyes, and disdainful of the judgment of crowds like her suit whose outline defied the lines of her body and whose neckline only seemed able to be held closed at the price of a difficult movement of her arms.

Before her mother had had time to introduce the new arrival, Felicia got up and pulled Michele into a corner of the room where they couldn't be heard.

"I've got a man for you!" she said with an expression of satisfaction at an accomplished mission.

Michele couldn't help laughing.

"What news! It sounds like an announcement. Who is he?"

"He's an Italian, very handsome. I've known him for a long time, but I wasn't sure that he was what you need. I've thought about it and decided that he's perfect! You must meet him without losing a moment's time!"

This note of urgency, so like Felicia, cheered Michele up again. She wasn't at all certain that the candidate, whoever he was, was "what she needed," but she didn't want to disappoint her tutor. She did her best to show interest in the project, for lack of gratitude for her Felicia's concern.

"What does your young man look like?" she asked.

"Just like a Florentine marquis. I'm sure you've never met anyone as handsome. Tall, thin, with the nose of an eagle, black piercing eyes, a dark complexion, a strong face . . ."

"Well!"

"What? Don't believe me if you prefer. But I'm sure that you won't laugh so stupidly when you see him. He's also born under the sign of the Lion."

"Who else is?"

"Diane and I!"

"Oh, well then . . ."

"But he has black shiny hair like yours, with just enough silver in it to be chic."

"Grey hair! Then he's an old man!"

"Naturally. He's the right age for you exactly—double yours, thirty-eight. That's why I'm telling you that you have to hurry: next year, you'll be too old. Anyway, he won't be here anymore next year."

"What is he doing in Bangkok?"

"Nothing. He's very intelligent. He knows everything. He goes through the ruins, he studies the age of the buddhas. He even found things at the museum that the guard there never saw. I think he's writing a book or something. But, as I told you, he doesn't do anything in particular."

Michele interrupted Felicia quickly:

"Tell me, who is that fantastic girl?

"Fantastic girl?"

"Yes, the one who just came in."

"Came in where?"

"Why *here*, Felicia! Have you become stupid? There, look, right in front of you . . ."

"Are you talking about Fay?"

"Oh, is that her name? How do you spell that?"

"What's the difference? It's just a silly English name."

"Is she English?"

"No, American. But she speaks French very well."

"You don't seem to like her."

"She's my best friend!"

"Well, why haven't you told me about her?"

"I can't tell you about all the girls I know."

"But if you love her so much, you might at least have mentioned her to me."

"What makes you think I love her? She's my friend, that's all. She's not necessarily someone I love."

"Felicia! . . . How do you expect anyone to understand anything from the way you talk? The truth is that you don't want to tell me anything about what concerns you. And you don't want me to know your friends. Are you jealous or something? Are you afraid I'll take them away from you?"

"I don't understand how it would help you to waste your time with a bunch of girls."

"You make me laugh! My time isn't so precious. To listen to you, someone might think that my days are numbered!"

"Well!"

Felicia seemed to take it so seriously that

Michele was troubled by it. Michele protested: "I don't feel that I'm decrepit yet."

"Oh, you know how quickly that comes."

"And does this Fay also have one foot in the grave according to your calculations?"

"She'd twenty-two and a half."

"Is she married?"

"Not yet."

"Than she's even worse off than I am!"

Felicia did not comment.

"If I understand you, you have no intention of introducing me to her," said Michele.

"Well all you had to do was ask me instead of talking stupidly."

Felicia waved to Fay who walked over to join them.

"This is Michele," said Felicia as she would have announced someone guilty of a crime.

The big grey eyes seen up close gave an impression of intelligence and freedom.

They exchanged some inoffensive banalities. The girl's voice went well with her looks. She never hesitated and there was an intimate gaiety about it which made Michele think that this woman had a sound of happiness.

She wanted to know how Fay occupied her days. Walking through the city mostly, it seemed. Did she live alone in Bangkok? No, she had come to visit her brother a year ago. He was a naval attaché to the American Embassy. At first she had only intended to remain a month but she was still here. She was in no hurry to go away now.

"When I've had enough of this prolonged vacation," she said, "I'll get married and return to the United States. I don't want to work. I adore having nothing to do."

"Are you engaged?" asked Michele.

This question allowed her to discover Fay's laugh. It was very open and pretty.

"You know, in my country, you get engaged on the eve of your marriage and the night before you still don't know with whom. Since it's neither tomorrow or the day after that that I intend to retire, I would find it very difficult to tell you what choice I will make."

"But getting married isn't necessarily retiring," protested Michele.

Fay smiled indulgently. She said simply; "Oh . . ." with a doubtful intonation. She added: "Retiring isn't such a bad thing."

Michele wanted to ask: retire from what? But she was afraid of being indiscreet. It was Fay who continued:

"Are you happy to have married so young?"

"Oh, yes!" said Michele. "It's the smartest thing I've ever done in my life."

Fay smiled again. Michele was seized by the impression of goodness that emanated from her. The beauty of her face, which was almost disturbing in its perfection, was forgotten as soon as the playfulness pierced through her like the sun through a stained-glass window. You no longer wanted to say: how beautiful this woman is! but: how sympathetic she is! Michele, however, preferred to think: how happy she seems! She felt that this state brought them together because she was conscious that she herself was happy. And misfortune frightened her to the point that she was incapable of sincerely loving anyone who was suffering either from sickness, poverty, or oppression. At times she was ashamed of this facet of her nature, although it didn't denote a hardness of her heart, but only a suspicious, almost obsessive passion for beauty.

While Felicia was making conversation with the ladies, Michele never left Fay. They were talking about unimportant things, but it was clear that they both found it pleasant to be together. Michele was even happy enough that her little friend was neglecting her. When David came to get her, she was sorry to have to leave. Felicia threw her an "I'll call you!" in a busy tone of voice when she said goodbye. Michele thought later that she should have asked Fay's telephone number. She was so worried about this omission that she couldn't answer her husband's questions.

* * *

Michele, without being able to explain exactly why to herself, was afraid to see Diane again. Rather than risk meeting her at the Sports Club, she renounced her morning swim. She had asked her husband what he thought of the young countess and he had answered that he found her very beautiful. He liked her spirit and her absence of affected manners. Had he made love to her, Michele had wanted to know. No, but, if the occasion had presented itself, he would have liked to. Michele, who was generally rather proud that her husband had been successful with other women, this time felt—against all logic, since in fact he hadn't been with Diane—a violent attack of jealousy, which she forced herself to hide from David, but which seemed to poison her whole day.

A little after this conversation, she received a call from Diane. She said that she was bored with the rain that had been falling for six days but she had just had a "nice idea." She was going to teach Michele squash. What was that? A kind of tennis that you could even play when it rained because it was done under a roof. Michele was going to love it. Diane would bring the rackets and balls, and all that Michele had to do was to put on some shorts, find some tennis shoes, and meet her at the Club in half an hour.

The countess hung up before Michele had time to make up an excuse. She reflected that, after all, this sport which she had heard so much about *would* be amusing, and she got ready to go.

When they met at the club, the two women discovered that they were dressed in the same way: yellow cotton pullovers over black shorts. They laughed loudly.

"Are you wearing a bra?" asked Diane.

"Never," admitted Michele. "I don't own a single one."

"Wonderful!" said her companion, seizing her by the waist and lifting Michele off the ground. She would never have imagined that Diane was so strong.

Diane proclaimed:

"Don't believe a word of all that gossip on the subject of tennis or horseback riding making your breasts fall if you don't tie them up in those malicious bags. It's just the opposite.

Sports strengthen them and the harder a life you lead, the more firm they become. You should see mine!"

She lifted her shirt right out in the open where there were other players. Michele was not the only one who was able to admire the woman's bust.

She found that, from first glance, a squash-court was the most common thing in the world: a floor, four wood partitions, and a roof. From the gallery from which she first saw it, it appeared like a kind of pit to her. They went down a ladder which turned around its upper bar to lie flat against the roof, automatically raised by springs as soon as they had placed their feet on the ground. To leave the pit they had to bring the ladder down again by pulling on a rope. Diane explained that the game consisted of each of them taking turns at hitting a hard rubber ball against the partition, using a racket with a small diameter and a long handle.

The little black ball flew so quickly under Diane's smashes that Michele had to run like a madman from one wall to the other, laughing loudly when her hair blew in her face. After a half-hour, she was returning the balls brilliantly, but her legs were crumbling under her and she was out of breath. Her body was completely shiny. Diane gave a signal for them to rest and brought down the ladder. She pulled two towels out of a sack she had tied to the bars. She removed her sweater and rubbed herself energetically, then went over to Michele and used a dry towel to sponge her friend's chest and back which Michele allowed her to do, panting all the while. Her wet pullover was rolled under her arms and she didn't have the courage to lift her arms to take it off. Diane leaned against the ladder on which Michele was pretending to be crucified, her arms and legs apart.

Her partner rubbed her breasts lightly and she continued well after they were dry. To the violent sensations of breathlessness, of fatigue, and of thirst which were burning Michele's larynx, had been added a congestion which was not completely disagreeable. Suddenly, Diane let the towel fall and, sliding her arms under those of her pupil, she stretched her whole body against her. Michele felt the tips of Diane's breasts seeking hers (as soon as they had found her, she abandoned herself to the pleasure, too great for her to be able to resist) and an active pubis which was pressing her through the material of her shorts. Her position made up for the few inches difference in their heights so that their mouths were exactly at the same level. Diane kissed her as Michele had never been kissed: very deeply, exploring without neglecting the slightest surface of her lips, her tongue, all the outlines and curves of her mouth, her palate, and her teeth. She no longer felt the thirst which had been irritating her throat a while ago. She moved gently so that her clitoris could expand, harden, and seek refuge in the solidity of the other abdomen. When the erection was so strong that Michele was no more than an enormous bud ready to burst, she pressed one of Diane's thighs between her legs without even being aware of it and began to rub her cunt against it in a supple movement with her whole body. Diane let her do this for several minutes, knowing that Michele needed this outlet for the excessive tension of her senses. Then she withdrew her lips and looked at her protégé with that laughing expression she had so often used and which seemed to be from joy at having told a good joke. Michele was troubled and reassured by this at the same time, noticing that Diane was putting very little feeling into their embraces. She wanted to be kissed again—and she didn't want Diane's breasts to leave her. But Diane took her by the hips as she had done earlier when they had first arrived, and, with an athletic movement, lifted her along the ladder. Michele's heels clung to the bar. She thought that Diane wanted to kiss her breasts, but the game leader kept her head at a distance and her laughing eyes never left those of her victim. Before Michele had time to get a clear idea of what had happened, Diane's hand was insinuating its way through the legs of her shorts and had already taken possession of her humid cunt.

Diane's fingers were as skillful, practiced, and efficacious as her tongue. They caressed her clitoris then plunged deeply into her flesh, pushing aside the walls, caressing the resistant protuberance of her womb, and displaying admirable activity and judgment.

Michele let herself be led to an orgasm without resistance, opening herself and stretching toward the hand that was caressing her. She had the feeling that a lava was being unleashed in her and was flowing, thick and warm, along Diane. When she finally slid along the ladder, her friend gathered her in her arms and pressed her against her body. If Michele had been able to see Diane's eyes at that moment, she might perhaps have been surprised to discover that they were no longer laughing.

* * *

However, when Michele came to herself again, her partner had regained her mischievousness and her customary warmth. She held her by the shoulders at arm's length. She burst out laughing and asked, gently:

"Do you have enough strength to climb the ladder?"

Michele suddenly experienced an intense confusion and lowered her face like a sullen child. The other girl took her chin between her fingers and lifted it. She was very close again.

"Tell me," she murmured in a serious, almost inaudible tone, which Michele had never known her to use, "have other women done that to you already?"

Michele remained impassive outside, but, in truth, her mind was prey to a confusion which she herself found it difficult to understand. She pretended not to hear. However, Diane insisted, imperious and coaxing at the same time:

"Answer! Have you ever made love with women?"

Michele remained silent. Diane moved closer and her lips brushed against those of her friend.

"Come to my house," she whispered. "Would you like that?"

But Michele shook her head negatively.

Diane kept the rebellious chin in her hand for a long moment, but she said nothing else. When she finally moved away, nothing in her eyes and her expression revealed whether she had been disappointed by Michele's refusal and whether she was angry or not.

"Climb," she said, after having caressed her with the end of her nose.

Michele turned around and climbed the ladder. Diane followed her. Michele lowered her sweater over her waist.

"Oh, you left your sweater down there!" she remarked. And she immediately offered: "Do you want me to go and get it?"

But Diane waved her hand disdainfully:

"Leave it! It's not worth the trouble. It's completely ruined."

She threw a towel over her shoulders without worrying about crossing it over her chest. She balanced the rackets and her bag in one hand as they both walked toward the garage. With the other, she held Michele's hand. Groups of people waved to her in passing, and she returned their salute gaily, uncovering the nudity of her breasts a little more each time. Michele suddenly had the impression that the whole world was watching her. She no longer felt anything but modesty and alarm. She was in a hurry to leave Diane and was once again determined not to see her anymore.

When they reached their cars, Diane let go of her companion's hand and faced her, while she finally tied the ends of her towel in front of her. She looked at her with a questioning and expectant expression whose ironic eloquence had no need of words. Again, Michele lowered her head. Her embarrassment and the disorder of her thoughts was not feigned. Diane did not insist. She leaned over and kissed her friend lightly on the cheek.

"See you soon, honey," she said lightly.

She jumped into her car and drove off, waving her hand.

When she had left, Michele regretted not having done anything to keep her from leaving. She would like to have seen her breasts again. She would have liked especially to have felt them on her again. She suddenly wanted to be naked and to have Diane naked and stretched out all along her, both of them naked, more naked than she had ever been. She wanted those breasts against hers and Diane's cunt against her own. And she wanted to be caressed by the woman's hands, by her legs, her lips, by a *woman's* body. If Diane had come back at that moment, oh how Michele would have given herself to her!

* * *

Paul arrived the same day. He was much more handsome than his photos. He had the open laugh of an English rugby player. His blond hair was poorly combed and seemed to be struggling against air currents. Michele immediately felt friendly toward him just as she would have felt with an old friend. Showing him her gardens, she put one arm in her husband's, and the other in Paul's.

She told David:

"You're not going to make Paul work all the

time! I want to take him to the khlongs, show him the thieve's market . . ."

"But I'm not here on vacation," said Paul, enchanted.

The double pleasure of seeing David and of finding him so well married gave the most favorable glow to this Sunday. He did not hide the admiration which Michele inspired.

"That devil David is really too lucky!" he cried, showering his hostess with an enthusiastic expression. "He never did anything to deserve you!"

"Fortunately," she joked. "I would hate a deserving husband!"

They were up late, only going to bed when sleep triumphed over Michele, closing her eyes in the armchair in which she was lodged, under the bougainvillea which covered the ground-level terrace. It wasn't raining, and the frogs were quiet. The middle of August often offered this deceptive respite.

* * *

Michele slept in the nude, but in order to have breakfast with David on the large balcony of their room, she put on one of those little nightgowns that was very short and of which (in part for the pleasure of trying them on) she had acquired a great number before her departure from Paris. The one she was wearing this morning was transparent and pleated and the color was almost identical with that of her skin. The hem barely covered her pubis. Three buttons secured it around her waist. The slightest breeze lifted it. Michele suddenly began to laugh.

"Good God! I forgot that we have a guest. I'd better put something on that's a little more covered."

And she hurried to change. But David intervened:

"Absolutely not," he said. "You look much better like that."

She did not object to showing herself this way, accustomed to being seen naked by all sorts of people. In this respect, her husband's attitude prolonged that of her childhood. The idea that she had to put on a robe to appear before them would have been absurd to her parents as well as to her. She had bought nightgowns after her marriage out of coquettery and not modesty.

Paul was less at ease than his hosts. Sitting in front of Michele, he couldn't take his eyes off her breasts which the sun was animating through the pleats. The nipples looked like tiny drops of blood. When she got up and brought him the biscuits, fruits and honey, the morning breeze half-opened the lingerie to her navel and the Persian lamb triangle came over to him —so close to his face that he could breath its perfume.

He did not dare bring a cup of tea to his lips for fear that his hands would tremble. He thought wildly: "What will happen if I have to get up? Or if someone comes to take the tablecloth away?"

Michele fortunately returned to her room before the men had finished eating. Paul thus had time to get hold of himself.

* * *

She didn't have to be back until dinner time. Michele didn't want to stay home alone all day. She took her car and left for the center of the city. She drove aimlessly for an hour, often wandering around, often stopping to enter a store, and then losing herself in the horrified contemplation of a leper. He was sitting on the ground, and he moved backwards, leaning on his wasted wrists and dragging his stumps of thighs over the dirty ground. Michele was so overcome by this spectable that she couldn't make the car go forward. She stayed there, paralyzed, having forgotten where she wanted to go and the maneuvers she had to make. At that moment, she recognized a silhouette not far off, coming out of a Chinese boutique. She let out a cry which resounded like a call for help:

"Fay!"

The young girl turned around and made a gesture of joyous surprise. She walked over to the car.

"I was looking for you," said Michele.

At the same time, she realized that it was true.

"Well, you were lucky to have found me," joked Fay, "because I don't come to this side very often."

"Of course, she doesn't believe me," Michele thought sadly.

"Would you like to have lunch together?" she proposed in an entreating voice so insistent that Fay didn't know how to answer for a moment.

It was Michele who pursued:

"I've got an idea! Come to my house. It's full of things to eat. And you still haven't seen my house."

"Wouldn't you prefer that I make you try out one of the local curiosities?" offered Fay. "There's a little Siamese restaurant near here that's very picturesque. I'll take you there."

"No, no!" Michele persisted. "Another time. Now that I've found you, I want to bring you with me."

"If you wish!"

Michele relaxed. She suddenly had the feeling of having found herself again, sure of her desires, proud of what she loved, as incapable of pretending as she was of waiting. It would have taken very little else to make her cry her joy out at the top of her lungs, while she was driving, despite all prudence, through the city's crowds. She laughed periodically without pretext. She seemed to be emitting rays of light. A song of hope ran through her head. "Oh my firm earth! Oh my beauty of winged delight, oh you, my beauty, my sweet beauty! O my earth of winged delight, oh my beauty, my sweet beauty! My promised beauty of winged delight, my beauty, oh my sweet beauty!"

She held out her arms tenderly, like a shipwrecked person, shaking her wavy hair. At last, at last! She sobbed with happiness at the sight of the beautiful shore of this sweet earth. How soft the ground was on which the waves deposited her, so sweet to her torso and naked legs, so welcoming to her liberated body. Everything was forgotten of what she had learned since she had come from one world to another in the sorcery of an August night. The dawn of forever was gilding her lips.

Fay looked at her with admiration and a little perplexity.

She liked the elegance and the modernism of the decoration. She admired the floral arrangements, a Japanese talent which Michele had acquired in Paris; the ceramic objects, the translucent stone basins garnished with coral and seashells; and the big wrought iron mobile that stood up in the middle of the room, encumbering, provocative, clanking with all its unusual iron foliage.

They lunched rapidly. Michele was very quiet. Her eyes never left her guest.

Then they visited the garden, despite the burning sun. Michele was guiding her friend by the hand through the cuttings and the shoots to make her sense what the beauty of the country would be when her shrubs had flowered.

She cut a rose with a long stem and held it out to Fay. The girl surrounded the red corolla with her fingers and placed it against her cheek. Michele came closer and gave the rose a kiss.

When they returned to the house, the sweat was clinging to their faces and necks.

"Would you like to take a shower?" suggested Michele.

Fay agreed that it was a good idea.

As soon as they were in her room, Michele pulled off her clothes as quickly as if they had been on fire. Fay only began to undress when

Michele had taken off the last piece of her suit. She was the first to say:

"What a beautiful body you have!"

Then she slowly undid her collar. When she had half-opened her blouse which she was wearing directly over her skin, Michele could not hold back an exclamation: Fay's chest was just like that of a boy.

"You see how flat I am," said the young girl.

She didn't seem in the least bit humiliated. She was savoring Michele's surprise. The lady of the house inspected the rosy nipples that were so tiny and so pale that they appeared pre-pubescent. Fay asked:

"Do you find them ugly?"

"Oh, no! On the contrary, they're marvelous!" cried Michele with such a tone of fervor that the girl seemed touched by it.

"You have such admirable breasts," she remarked. "We offer an astonishing contrast, don't we?"

But Michele was fanatic:

"What's so interesting about having big breasts?" she said. "You only see that on magazine covers. But you're so different from other women. It's so pretty!'

Her voice softened a little:

"You know, I've never seen such exciting breasts. I'm not telling you that to be kind."

"No, but it amuses me," said Fay, who was sliding her skirt over her legs. "Perhaps I wouldn't mind having too small a bosom, but no breasts at all, that's funny, don't you think? (She suddenly seemed more loquacious. Michele couldn't remember ever having heard her utter such a long speech.) For a long time I've even lived in the fear of seeing my breasts begin to grow. I would have felt I was losing my whole personality. And I pray every night: 'My God, never let me have true breasts!' I've been so good that God has granted my wish!"

"What luck!" cried Michele. "It would have been terrible if your breasts had grown any larger. I love you so much like this!"

She found Fay's legs admirable as well, so long and slender that they seemed to come from the portfolio of a modern artist and were not completely real. The narrow hips and the flexible tiny waist added to the impression of slenderness and grace. But what struck Michele even more was when Fay had taken off her panties and she saw the extraordinary protuberance of her shaven pubis. She had never seen one whose relief detached itself so much from the abdominal plane, nor one which was as filled with female sexuality. She thought that she knew of none more beautiful in all the world nor more worthy of being loved. The absence of hair disencumbered the groove of her cunt which rose high and sank in deep and clean—offered to the world without evasion. The contrast with the non-existent bust and the fact that Fay's body was uniformly tanned (so that one could only think that it had been exposed completely to the sun and that others had been able to contemplate this hermaphroditic nudity at their ease) had something of a challenge about it. And, despite Fay's distant grace, the smooth and cloven swelling of her abdomen was so sensual, thrown forward with such an inviting movement, that Michele felt her own cunt touched as if by a hand. Fay would have to belong to her immediately, she realized. That voluptuous furrow had to be opened to her—oh! that slit! That slit—the sight of which made her tremble. She opened her mouth to tell Fay what she wanted, but at the same moment, the young girl turned toward the bathroom.

"The shower?" she recalled.

The artifice seemed superfluous to Michele now. In order to cut short Fay's movement, she ordered:

"Come here on the bed."

The visitor stopped before the door with a hesitant attitude, then began to laugh.

"But I want to refresh myself, not sleep," she said.

Michele wondered if Fay really believed that she had received an invitation to a siesta or whether she was only pretending innocence. She exchanged glances with her nude friend and despaired when she found no hint of teasing in the girl's eyes.

She rejoined Fay and opened the door:

"Well then, we'll make love under the shower," she said frankly.

CHAPTER FOUR

The huge white bathroom was equipped with several kinds of showers. One was fixed to the wall and another to the ceiling, a third smaller one was at the end of a long curled pipe that could be held in the hand and aimed in any direction. Close to one another under the crossing rains, the two women uttered chilled cries. In order to protect her hair, Michele had pushed it on top of her head and this edifice made her seem as tall as her companion.

She told Fay that she was going to show her how to use the flexible shower. She took the pipe in her right hand, put her left arm around her friend's hips and ordered her to open her legs.

Fay smiled and obeyed. Michele directed the warm flow of water obliquely up and down toward her guest's cunt, then brought it closer and closer, now imprinting a light trembling, now a spiral movement. She seemed to know the rules of the game very well. The water fell in cascades between Fay's legs. Michele raised her eyes.

"Is it good?" she asked.

Fay seemed to find the question incongruous. She hesitated a moment, seemed to want to say something, changed her mind, then finally contented herself to nod her head affirmatively. An instant later however, she said:

"Yes, very good!"

Without ceasing to direct the shower, and with a sure hand, Michele leaned forward and took one of the little nipples in her mouth. She felt one of Fay's hands come to rest on her hair. Was it to push her away? Was it to press her to her? Michele squeezed the doll-like breast between her lips, provoking it with the tip of her tongue and sucking it. It became hard immediately, more than doubling in size. She stood up, triumphant.

"You see . . ."

But she stooped abruptly. Fay's features had lost their serene mask. The beautiful grey eyes were even more immense, the lips had augmented in thickness and luster. The almost childlike face—a face whom Michele had not known until now—was bursting with intensity and beauty. She came without a cry, without a shiver, without the rhythm of her body betraying the violence of her pleasure.

Her ecstasy lasted so long that Michele wondered whether her friend was still conscious of her presence. Then gradually the marvelous expression was wiped away and Michele was sad that the pleasure couldn't last any longer. She was so intimidated by the transfiguration she had witnessed that she didn't dare speak. Fay smiled at her.

Michele put her arms around her friend's neck and kissed her lips. She moaned with pleasure when Fay's body was welded to hers. The moist freshness of their two skins was like a caress. She held her tightly, slowly rubbing the girl's pubis against her own.

Fay guessed the pleasure Michele sought. She placed her hand on her hostess' buttocks, pressed gently on them, joining her to her belly. In her mouth was a strange taste that was sweet and juicy, like an exotic fruit. She felt the spasm which was rising in the beautiful body she held against her. She helped her as much as she could. She heard the murmuring of words which had the sound of love.

* * *

"Michele is intelligent, curious about everything, and always in a good mood. But that isn't why I married her," said David to Paul as they drove in the jeep.

Sweat was making their skin sticky and the heaviness of the air was inflaming their throats. They crossed a little bridge. Some boys and girls were playing naked in the water and splashing each other with howling laughter.

"Look. Isn't that the Orient of the movies?"

David stopped the motor and they went down to the fountain to refresh their faces. The children jumped with enthusiasm, pointing at them with their fingers, and squealing in a chorus:

"Farang! Farang!"

"What are they saying?" asked Paul.

"Just: 'Europeans! Europeans!' It's just like the idiots at home who cry; 'Chinese! Chinese!'"

A little girl whose wet hair was caressing her shoulders with long black tongues came over to them. She had picked up a blue sarong from the ground which contrasted with her amber skin and tied it around her waist as she walked.

"Than yâk sü som-ô mai tja?" she asked, addressing the foreigners with a charming smile.

"I don't know what she wants," confessed David.

The little girl pointed to a basket of enormous grapefruits placed in the shade of a tree.

"Oh, I see. She's offering us some fruit. It wouldn't be a bad idea."

David shook his head affirmatively, saying:

"Ao ko dai!"

The child ran to the basket and came back with a fruit that was bigger than her head. She raised her hand with her five fingers separated:

"Hâ baht."

"Alright, little one," said David.

He held out a bill which she examined carefully.

"Is our account in order?" asked David.

"Kha!"

She did not seem in the least disturbed by

this bilingual conversation. Paul was astonished.

"Does she speak French?"

"Not a bit. But that doesn't mean we can't understand each other."

The little girl lifted the fruit to her face with a questioning expression.

"Pok hai mai tja?"

David separated his arms as a sign of incomprehension. The child's free hand described imaginary circles around the fruit, then she made some peeling gestures.

"Oh, yes, why not?" said David. "That would be very nice of you."

She returned to her basket, took out a little knife then sat down with the fruit placed on her skirt.

The two men sat down on the grass across from her.

"Since you didn't marry Michele for her mind, as you say, I suppose it was because of her beauty," said Paul. "That's easy to understand."

"Perhaps, but that wouldn't have been enough to win me."

"Well then? What conquered you? Her homemaking talents?"

"No, her carnal nature. I don't know anyone in the world who likes to make love as much as she, or who does it as well."

Paul was shocked. This type of confession seemed in bad taste to him. However, he was burning to hear more about it.

"You're certainly lucky," he said with some effort. "But aren't you also running a risk? This . . . what would you call it? . . . this gift she has—wouldn't others guess it and be tempted . . . to try to profit by it . . . try to take her?"

"No one can take what doesn't belong to me," said David. "She's not my possession."

Paul's face reflected incomprehension. David added: "And I didn't marry her to deprive her."

The little girl held out the grapefruit sections. David took one and, after thanking her, swallowed it with manifest pleasure.

"Don't you want any?" he asked Paul.

The younger man took the offered fruit mechanically. There was an absent look in his eyes. David said again:

"Michele and I are interested in the world. And we have a desire to know more about it."

Then he laughed openly: "There's a lot to do!"

He took another piece of fruit from the child.

"Even for two," he concluded. "And enough to justify working as a team."

Paul wondered whether David's words had any bearing on himself. The children were crouching in a circle around them and watching them in silence, from time to time giggling and finally leaving in a burst of laughter that was making tears run down their cheeks.

"They're making fun of us," remarked Paul.

The sweet pulp had refreshed his tongue, but his throat had remained curiously tight. He tried to struggle against the images that were pushing their way into his head with a sweet insistance that horrified him.

"So," he thought, "that's the way I think about my friend's wife!"

But the vision persisted. He suggested that they buy some more fruit. But, while the little Siamese girl was preparing it and he was trying to talk about their work, his imagination kept conjuring up Michele's round breasts, her nervous legs, the tempting nudity of her belly. David jumped to his feet, announcing that the time had come for them to get back to work. Only then did he notice Paul's emotional state that was spectacular under his thin cotton shorts. He rounded his lips in surprise and burst out laughing:

"Well, I didn't know you had such a taste for little girls."

He pointed to their hostess who did not seem to understand the situation in the least.

"Listen," continued David, "at least wait until they're a little riper. This one's not even eight years old!"

* * *

Michele had wanted to wash her guest's body. She knew how to do it so well, sliding her hand between Fay's legs, but the girl tried to defend herself.

"No, no, not constantly, Michele! It's too tiring. Let me get my strength back."

Her friend allowed her to rinse and dry herself. Then she said: "Come to my bed!"

Fay did not answer at first. Then the young girl kissed her hostess on the eyelids.

"Let's got to your room," she said.

Michele put Fay across the big bed, stretched

out on her, and covered her forehead, her neck, and her chest with kisses. She let herself slide to the floor and, getting on her knees, buried her face in the naked belly.

"Oh," she moaned, "it's so soft!"

She rubbed her cheeks one after another then her nose and lips against the girl's protuberant pussy.

"Darling! Darling!"

Fay did not move and remained silent. Michele was worried.

"Are you alright like this?"

"Yes."

"Do you want to be my lover?"

"But, Michele . . ."

She stopped, caressed Michele's hair, and waited.

Michele's hands separated her long legs, rubbed the opening between them, and penetrated it gently. Fay sighed, let her arms fall, and closed her eyes. Michele brought the tip of her tongue to the narrow opening like a cock. She moistened the edges of the vulva, licked the inside, then sought the clitoris, sucked it, stimulated it, moistened it with saliva, and made it come and go between her lips like a tiny phallus. She slid her finger into her own vagina then with her free hand she continued to stimulate her friend's pussy. Her fingers were all wet. She moved them between the girl's buttocks. Fay lifted herself so that Michele could penetrate her narrow orifice more easily. The finger went all the way in. Only then did Fay cry. She continued to cry all the time that Michele licked her, sucked her and moved her hand from one opening to the other. It was

Michele who had to admit she was tired first. She stretched out on top of her mistress again. Neither seemed to have the strength to talk.

Later, when Fay, despite Michele's begging, had already dressed again, her hostess put her arms around her and forced her to sit down on the bed again.

"I want you to tell me something. But swear that you'll tell me the truth!"

Fay smiled and nodded affirmatively.

Michele said:

"I love you."

Fay looked deep into the golden eyes for a clue to what she should answer, for what sort of truth was expected of her. But Michele's grave, almost pathetic expression had already been replaced by a wheedling one. She placed her cheek on her friend's shoulder.

"Are you sure you like me? I mean, no, wait, listen to me first, do I please you as much or more than any of your other girlfriends? Did I give you as much pleasure?"

This time, Fay laughed frankly. Michele was angry.

"Why are you making fun of me?" she cried.

"Listen, little Michele," murmured Fay, and she brought her lips very close to hers. "I'm going to tell you a big secret. I've never done what we did this afternoon before."

"You mean the shower, the . . ."

"Everything! I've never made love with another woman."

"Oh!" protested Michele. "I don't believe you!"

"You have to believe me since it's true. And I'm going to tell you something else. Until this afternoon, until I knew you, I even found something like this a little ridiculous."

"But . . ." Michele stammered, "do you mean you don't like doing it?"

"I never even tried it."

"That's impossible," cried Michele in such a way that Fay burst out laughing.

"Why? Did I seem so experienced?" asked Fay in an almost joking tone of complicity which was quite new from her lips and disconcerted Michele.

"You don't seem surprised."

"I wasn't because it was with you."

Michele thought for a moment, then as if she was coming out of a dream, as if she had forgotten the whole preceding conversation, she asked:

"Don't you love me, Fay?"

The girl looked at her without smiling.

"Yes, I love you."

Michele was expecting something else. She asked another question, less because she attached any importance to it than to break the silence:

"And . . . did you like the experience? Are you happy?"

Fay's face suddenly had a resolute expression.

"This time," she said, "I'm going to caress you."

Michele didn't have time to answer. Fay took her by the waist and forced her to lie down. She kissed her cunt as she would have kissed her mouth. She leaned her head sideways so that her own lips would be parallel to these other lips. She put her tongue out, sliding it into the soft slit as far as possible. Michele felt submerged in love and desire at the same time. Fay wasn't able to try any other caresses. Surprised by the suddenness of Michele's orgasm, she recoiled at first. But when she saw that Michele was continuing to be shaken by shivers, she applied her mouth again and licked the juice which was flowing from her lover. When she sat up she said, laughing:

"I never would have thought that someday I'd love drinking from this fountain! Well, now you see that I love you."

The ringing of the telephone broke the charm. It was Felicia announcing her visit. Ordinarily, Michele would have been delighted. At this moment the news shocked her. It took all of Fay's good humor to overcome her misery. They didn't want to confront Felicia together so they agreed to meet the next day. Fay would come to Michele's house in the morning. The chauffeur would drive her home.

Michele waited for her visitor without even bothering to put on her clothes. The surprising thing was that at the moment she didn't have the least intention of corrupting her little friend.

She was too incapable of disguising her emotions for Felicia's perspicacity not to be immediately alerted, however.

"What happened to you?" she asked. "You're acting like a girl who's just had a marriage proposal."

Michele tried to elude the truth but it didn't take long for her young friend to elicit it from her.

"I've great news for you that's going to

interest you," she finally announced. "Prepare yourself to be amazed."

"You're pregnant?"

"Don't be stupid. Try to guess."

"No, tell me. What are you babbling about?"

"Nothing. What I have to tell you is that I just made love to Fay."

Michele was not at all sure of the effect her words would produce. However, she wasn't expecting Felicia's reaction to be so discouraging.

"Is that all you have to tell me?" asked the young girl in a blasé tone of voice. "That wasn't worth a whole preamble. What's extraordinary about that?"

"But . . ." said Michele miserably. "Fay is fascinating. Don't you think she is?"

Felicia shrugged her shoulders.

"Poor Michele! You can be so silly. I really don't see what glory there can be about going to bed with a girl. You announced it like it's a great achievement or something—you make me laugh!"

Michele was vexed. She was starting to feel guilty. But of what? She tried to see it more clearly.

"I wonder what's bothering you. What do you have against Fay and me making love?"

Felicia delivered the following edict in a very definitive tone of voice:

"You don't make love with a woman," she said.

"Oh?" said Michele.

"You make love with a man."

She added in a tone of weary authority: "I already told you that I know someone capable of teaching you. Since talking doesn't seem to have any effect on you, the best thing is for me to put you in Gino's hands without delay."

She seemed to be consulting a calender mentally.

"Today's the sixteenth. I suppose you're invited to the embassy on the eighteenth? Good. I'll take advantage of that reception to introduce you to him. If you can't arrange to make love to him that night, it'll have to be the next day."

* * *

She couldn't stand waiting any longer. She was on her knees on an armchair with her elbows resting on the balcony, her chin in her hands, scrutinizing the street. Her lips were trembling with anxiety. Would she come? Why was she so late? Perhaps she was going to find an excuse not to see Michele. Would she call?

When the hours had passed and waiting had become too painful, Michele finally decided to telephone. It was after twelve. A man's voice answered the number Fay had given her. No doubt it was a servant. Suddenly Michele realized that she didn't know what to say because of her ignorance of the language. She gave Fay's name and her own to the servant, but she didn't know whether he understood. She hung up.

Since Fay hadn't answered herself, did it mean that she was on her way? Then she might arrive at any moment. Michele took up her post again. What if she'd had an accident? Another idea came to Michele: perhaps Fay couldn't find the house and was wandering around looking for it all this time through the labyrinth of the residential quarters. All the streets looked alike, their names were unpronounceable and written in Siamese characters. There was nothing surprising about her getting lost.

All the same, a stronger voice objected in Michele's mind: in the year that Fay had lived in Bangkok, she must have learned to know all the detours. Hadn't even she learned how to get around after only two weeks? How could she believe that Fay could have gotten lost? Anyway, it was two hours after she'd promised to be here. If she'd forgotten where Michele lived, what would stop her from calling to tell her or to ask her to come and get her?

In fact, why shouldn't she go to Fay's house? Then she realized that she'd forgotten to ask the young girl for her address. Felicia had said she was the sister of an American naval attaché. That was a little vague. Anyway, Michele wasn't about to call the United States Embassy to find out. But why not, after all? What name would she ask for? There could have been several naval attachés. And what language would she speak?

The chauffeur who had taken Fay home! Trembling with impatience, Michele had him called. They couldn't find him. No doubt he had gone to lunch.

How stupid she'd been! Why hadn't she thought about it before? All she had to do was call Felicia. But as soon as the idea came to her, she recoiled. Was she going to tell the little girl with the green eyes that she was waiting for Fay and thus expose herself to new sarcasms? Her wounded pride forbade her to let Felicia guess that Fay wasn't on time for their date, that perhaps Michele's amorous fervor was not returned and that her tender mistress of the previous day was already unfaithful.

Michele was certain now that Fay would never come back. She wouldn't come back later or tomorrow. Yesterday she had given in to an enchantment that was stronger than her, but, away from Michele's presence, she had come to herself. She didn't love her, she didn't love women. It seemed absurd and boring to her. In her own words, it was "ridiculous." Or else she was ashamed of having given in to the pleasures of the flesh. Michele thought that Fay no doubt had religious beliefs, or a moral conception that had made her repent for the pleasure she had taken. After all, Michele knew nothing about her. She lived alone, probably without a lover, since she lived with her brother.

Unless . . . the inverse hypothesis took its turn in Michele's mind: perhaps Fay had another mistress? Perhaps she had lied yesterday? No, Michele couldn't believe that. Or, perhaps, a lover to whom she had to confess her "sin" to and who was jealous, had made a scene, and demanded that she renounce Michele. That was it! Michele was convinced. But she wouldn't let herself be conquered that easily! She would fight to get her back—she had the power of love on her side . . .

The next instant had for Michele nothing but weakness and pain. A strange bitterness was gradually submerging everything that remained of her confidence. Fay would never come back, she would never see her again. What difference did the reasons make? The only thing that counted was Michele's solitude and misery. She loved her so much! She felt as though she had come to this country at the end of the world just to find her. When she had met her it had been as though she had been waiting for her always. She would have followed her wherever she had led her. She would have left everything for her if that had been her wish. But Fay would never ask anything. And Michele would never again be able to offer her what she had been ready to give. Yes, she would wipe away her memory! She would forget that face and that fiery hair, she would forget the soft voice saying:

"I love you too."

For the first time since she was small, real tears flowed down Michele's face, wetting her lips and tongue, falling over the balcony. She couldn't stop herself. Michele cried and held out her arms—and in vain turned toward the opening in the garden where in an instant, that night, perhaps tomorrow, no matter when, when it pleased her, Fay would appear and call to her . . .

* * *

That night David and Paul took her to the theatre. She didn't know what she was seeing. Her face reflected her pain. Her husband didn't dare ask questions. Paul, who didn't understand anything that was happening, looked almost as sad as Michele. When she was in David's arms in bed she cried again. She felt a little relieved. She confessed her unhappy love to him with less sobbing.

David was of the opinion that Michele was taking her adventure too tragically. In the first place, nothing proved that Fay's defection wasn't due to circumstances beyond her control and that she wouldn't appear the next day with a perfectly valid excuse. If it was true that she didn't want to see Michele again, what of it! It meant she wasn't worth the trouble she was causing. It was preferable that their union stop immediately because she certainly only had deceptions and more serious grief in store for Michele. Anyway, Michele had to think of herself as one who was courted and not one who ran after others. No matter how beautiful Fay—whom David had never seen and of whom he had never heard before —might be, he was certain that she couldn't possess a fourth of the grace or the qualities of his wife. Thus he couldn't permit her to humiliate herself to the girl. The only response that the unfaithful girl deserved if she thought she could mete out her favors to Michele, was for Michele to take her revenge in other arms. Michele wouldn't have trouble finding other partners who would be more worthy of her. She had to prove it to Fay immediately.

She listened quietly. He's right, she thought, without her pain being really appeased by it. To the extent, however, to which she accepted it, it was only to hear another Michele speaking of consoling herself or of avenging herself. Michele was a little confused by her distress. Perhaps it was simply the effects of sleepiness. She never knew whether her last thought before losing consciousness had been for the fugitive lover or for those, still without faces, who would one day replace her.

* * *

None of the dresses Michele had had made in France were cut low enough for David's tastes.

"But I'm the woman in Paris who shows the most of her breasts!" she had protested laughingly.

"What Paris calls showing the breasts is still too modest in Bangkok," her husband had said. "Everyone must know that you have the prettiest breasts in the world. The surest way to convince them is to put them in front of their eyes."

The dress which Michele wore to the reception at the Embassy fulfilled this function perfectly. The round neckline which clung to the low shoulders emphasized the beauty of Michele's neck by its large curve, only covering her nipples. When she leaned forward a little or sat down, her entire bosom appeared. Besides, the material was so thin and clung so tightly to her skin that any underwear would have shown through. Therefore, Michele had nothing on under the dress, not even one of her diaphanous panties. Since her marriage and even in Paris it was rare for her to put on panties when she dressed to go out at night. Feeling herself nude like that caused her a pleasure that was as physical as a caress. The sensation was even stronger if she had to dance of if she was wearing a very loose skirt.

Tonight her dress was as tight as a glove

at the waist but it quickly opened up at the bottom in a sort of spiral of surprising fullness. Michele let herself drop into a chair to show how this skirt lifted by itself, revealing her thighs. The spectacle that she offered was so gracefully immodest that David suddenly leaned over, searching under her arm for the invisible zipper which he lowered with a sure hand. With his other hand, he tried to remove his wife's naked body from its silk case.

"David," she protested, "what are you doing? You're mad! We'll be late. We have to leave immediately."

He stopped trying to undress her, lifted her off the ground, and stretched her out on the dining-room table.

"No! Oh no! My dress will be wrinkled. You're hurting me! What if Paul comes down? And the servants will see us!"

He placed her on her back so that her buttocks were on the edge of the table. She pulled on the material in order to uncover her abdomen as much as possible. Her legs were dangling and slightly bent. David, standing in front of her, penetrated her in a single blow. They both laughed at this suddenness. David's haste was bringing Michele a new pleasure which gave her throat the burning sensation that one has at the end of a long run. She squeezed the pulp of her breasts in her hands as if to make the nectar pour out. Her own caress made her delirious as much as the blows of her husband's rod. At her first cries, the native boy came running, thinking he had been called. He stopped, hesitating at the entrance to the room, his hands politely crossed in front of his chest. They must have heard Michele farther than the neighboring houses!

When David had put her on her feet again, he ordered the boy to clean the table which they had stained and called Michele's little maid so that she could help her mistress fix herself up. They were only a little late when they arrived at the Embassy.

The place was already crowded, however. The ambassador who had come to the end of his stay was giving this reception as a farewell party.

"Ravishing!" he cried before kissing Michele's hand. "My compliments, my dear!" He added to David: "I hope that your work leaves you some leisure time."

A lady with white hair whom she remembered having visited was watching the new guest with an expression of furious reprobation. Diane came in at that point to aggravate things.

"Why, unless my eyes are deceiving me," she cried, holding out her hands, "there's our little living public outrage on decency! Quick, let's introduce her to all our good swashbucklers!"

She attracted the attention of an elegant man who was conversing with a priest:

"Donald, look! What do you think of her?"

Michele prepared herself to confront the judgment of the adviser and that of the prelate at the same time. She felt that she managed the first test better than the second one. She had more or less expected Diane's husband to be a sort of pompous and monocled clown. Instead of that, the Count's first words made her burst out laughing and she found him very attractive physically.

Gentlemen of various ages were already surrounding her, offering her compliments and staring at her. But her attention was distracted. She was scrutinizing the unknown faces in the distance, wishing and fearing she would discover Fay. The entire diplomatic corps must have been there. Could they have invited her brother without inviting her? Perhaps so after all. Michele didn't know what her attitude would be if she suddenly found herself face to face with the young American. She hoped she wouldn't meet her. Each group seemed to be testing her. What had she come here to do? When would she be able to escape or at least find her husband's protection again?

He had been swallowed up by the crowd, however. Diane immediately seized Michele and led her into a whirlwind of introductions. The admiration of the men followed her everywhere. This courtship, to which she was accustomed, gave her confidence. Her face expressed indifference, but all those eyes that were undressing her warmed her at least as much as the cocktails which the Countess made her drink. Diane observed her in silence a long time while she was having a conversation with a group of flyers. She drew her aside quickly.

"You're magnificent!" she cried. (Her eyes were sparkling. She took the tip of one of her breasts between two fingers.) "Come with me into the parlor over there. There's no one else there!"

"No, no!" cried Michele.

Before Diane could stop her she ran away, rejoining the mass of guests, only feeling secure when an aging gentleman had accompanied her to the edge of the terrace under the pretext of admiring the Chinese lamps. Felicia discovered her engaged in this conversation.

"Excuse me, Commander," she said with her customary aplomb, "I have to talk to my friend."

She took Michele's arm without worrying about the man's protestations.

"What are you doing with that old creep?" she asked before they were hardly a few feet away. "I've been looking everywhere for you. Gino has been waiting for you for a good half-hour."

Michele had forgotten all about this date. She hardly felt up to it. Well, perhaps while the old man was flirting with her, she'd have some time to think about other things. Nevertheless, she tried to plead for her freedom.

"Is it really necessary?"

"Oh, listen Michele! (The young girl's voice had a worn-out tone.) Wait until you see him at least."

She sounded so comically full of promises that it returned Michele's good humor. Before she had time to scoff at the confidence that the little girl had in her hero's charms, he appeared before them.

"What a beautiful smile!" he said bowing. "How I wish it could have served as a model for the painters in my country. Don't you find that those controlled smiles, those Florentine suggestions, are merely grimaces? They deny art. I disapprove of anything that is controlled. In all the centuries in which art has been giving us the favors of its old imitations, it has really only existed in the truthfulness of an open face."

This entrance into the conversation floored Michele.

"Felicia wants to have me painted (she realized that the young girl hadn't even taken the pain to introduce them). Are you the artist whom she has judged worthy of this task?"

Gino smiled. Michele agreed that his smile had a rare grace.

"Even if I only possessed a grain of talent that I would allow myself to announce to the world, madame, I would offer it to you: the genius of the model would do the rest. Unfortunately, I don't even possess that much. I am rich only in the art of others."

Felicia intervened:

"He's a collector. You'll see! He has sculpture from this country and old things that he brought from Mexico, Africa, and Greece. Paintings . . ."

"Which only serve as immobile mementos of true art whose vitality challenges the dead figures. Felicia mia," he added, "don't believe in this bark fallen from the tree of life. I only keep them in memory of those who have suffered and been destroyed for pulling them from its trunk or from its branches, those who have been divested of breath and reason, of honor and life. At times it is the painter, but more often what he painted. Art is made up of the individual's loss. What is important is not the 'Portrait Ovale' but the painter's wife."

"When she's dead?" asked Michele.

"No, while she is dying."

"But did the painting come to life?"

"No! A small curiosity, at the very most an artifice. Art has only existed in what is lost: in the woman who died. Art was the death of her body. There can be no beauty in what is kept or in what subsists. Every born object dies."

"I have been taught the contrary," said Michele, "that good art alone has eternity."

"And who, I ask you, cares about eternity?" Gino interrupted violently. "Eternity isn't artistic, it's ugly. Its face is that of monuments to the dead. Its body is the cadaver of cities."

He wiped his temples with a fine handkerchief and continued in a more gentle tone:

"You know Goethe's cry: 'Stop, instant, you are so beautiful!' But if the instant were immobilized, that would be the end of its beauty! If one tries to eternalize beauty, the beauty dies. What is beautiful is not one who is nude, but one in the act of undressing. Not the sound of a laugh, but the chest laughing. Not the mark on the paper, but the moment when the artist's heart breaks."

"You said a moment ago that the artist was less important than the model."

"What I'm calling the artist is not necessarily the sculptor or the painter. The sculptor can be sometimes, if he takes his subject and undresses her. But more often the model accomplishes this task and the painter is only a witness."

"And where is the masterpiece?" asked Michele with sudden anxiety.

"The masterpiece is what happens. No, I didn't say that right. The masterpiece is what happened."

He took Michele's hand in his.

"Permit me to answer your earlier quote with another. 'The greatest work of art is not worthy of the smallest human life.' The only art that isn't futile is the history of the body."

"You mean that what is important is the way in which one lives? That you have to think of yourself as a work of art if you want to survive?"

"Yes, but if I had the least right to give you advice," said Gino in a courteous, slightly disdainful tone, "I wouldn't urge you just to survive. I would tell you to live."

He turned away. He seemed to feel that the conversation was over. Michele felt that her presence was no longer necessary. This was agreeable to her and she addressed herself to Felicia:

"Have you seen David by any chance? He disappeared the moment we arrived."

Other women surrounded the Italian. Michele profited by this and slipped away. But Felicia quickly caught up to her.

"So, you're keeping Fay locked up at your house," she said without seeming to attach too much importance to it. "Every time I try to call her, I remember that she's with you."

She let out a little gentle laugh:

"And as I don't want to interrupt you . . ."

Michele was thunderstruck. Was Felicia making fun of her? No, she seemed to believe what she was saying. What irony! Michele was on the point of screaming very loudly. Once again, human dignity held her back. Could she admit to Felicia that she had lost all trace of her lover? It would be better to keep up illusions that the little braided girl was making about the power of her elder. Unfortunately, Michele was depriving herself of a means of finding Fay by keeping quiet. She decided that she would ask Diane instead. But she couldn't see her short hair or hear her laughter anywhere. Had she found another victim to show her little parlor to?

Felicia was speaking about the American girl again.

"I wanted to tell her good-bye at least. Too bad for her—you tell her for me."

"What! She's going away?"

"No. I am."

"You? You didn't tell me. Where are you going?"

"Oh, don't worry—not far. I'm simply going to spend a month at the seaside. Mother rented a cottage. You'll have to come see us. It's not far, it's only thirty miles. You must see the beaches—they're marvelous!"

"I know. One of those wonderful places where the sharks come to eat out of your hand. I'll never see you again."

"Where did you pick up all that nonsense?"

"You're going to get bored there all alone."

Michele, to her own surprise, felt ready to cry. She would miss the girl, as unbearable as she was. But she didn't want her to see her sadness. She forced herself to laugh.

"I'll never get bored," her friend said. "I'll take sunbaths for hours and I'll water-ski. Anyway, I'll take a full valise of old books. I have to work again."

"That's true," said Michele, "I forgot that you had to go back to school."

"Not everyone has your innate knowledge."

"Won't you have any friends with you?"

"No, thanks. I want to be alone."

"You're very likeable! I hope your mother keeps an eye on you and doesn't let you run around with the fishermen's sons."

The green eyes produced an enigmatic smile.

"And you," said the young girl, "what are you going to do without me? You'll probably fall back on your natural stupidity!"

"Why no," teased Michele. "You know very well that I'm going to give myself to Gino."

Felicia seemed to instantly lose all desire to joke.

"You don't have to go back to that," she said. "You promised. Don't forget! You're no longer free."

"You're wrong there. I'll do what I want."

"Alright, provided that you want Gino. You don't intend to run away, I hope?"

Felicia looked so dejected that Michele was almost ashamed of herself. However she didn't want to show it.

"He's not as irresistible as you imagine. I find him a little foolish. He talks and listens to himself. He doesn't need an audience for reinforcement."

"Instead of being difficult to please, you should think of yourself as fortunate that a man like Gino is interested in you. You can tell yourself that he's the difficult one!"

"Oh really. And he's interested in me? That's quite an honor!"

"Exactly! All the same I was happy to see that you were making such a good impression on him. I can tell you that I wasn't exactly certain in advance."

"Thanks again. And from what, if you please, are you deducing the effect I had on him? I rather had the feeling that he was only interested in himself."

"I know him a little better than you. You'll admit that at least, won't you?"

"Of course! I presume that you have also accorded him your greatest favors for a long time. You might confess your impressions to me. That would help me not to appear too constrained at the hour of sacrifice."

"You'd be better off not acting so stupid if you don't want him to let you go. He hates stupidity."

Suddenly conciliating, Felicia added:

"But I know very well that in reality you're only putting on airs. Otherwise I wouldn't have introduced you to him."

Then, affectionate and coaxing:

"I'm sure that you're going to understand. You're going to be happy. And you'll be even more beautiful when I see you again. I want you always to be more and more beautiful."

Her expression had grown so sweet, that Michele was disturbed by it.

"Felicia," she murmured, "it's too bad that you're going away."

"We'll see each other soon. I won't forget you! Be well."

They exchanged a look of friendship, suddenly almost intimate. Then, Felicia regained control, as if to recover a ground which would lend itself less to tears.

"You promise again that you'll act like I told you with Gino, don't you?"

"Oh yes. Yes, if that will give you so much pleasure."

For the first time since they had known each other, Felicia brought her face close to Michele and placed a rapid kiss on her friend's cheek. Michele made a movement to hold her silky head against her, but the girl had already pulled away.

"See you soon, pussycat! I'll call you tomorrow before we leave. And you'll come see me at the sea."

"Yes," said Michele in a little voice.

"Now, let's go find the others."

They went to mingle with the crowd again. Michele passed from group to group, without letting herself become engrossed. She was looking for Diane. But it was the Countess who found Michele first.

"There you are again, immaculate virgin!" she cried. "I thought I'd lost you to some port of penitence."

"On the contrary," she answered in the same tone. "A Prince of Darkness was comparing my laugh to the art of the striptease."

"Who is this connoisseur?"

"I only know his first name is Gino. But you must know who he is . . ."

Diane laughed:

"Oh, that one. His jokes don't mean a thing! Your virtue would be more in danger if you were a pretty boy."

"You mean he's . . ."

"I would be afraid of slandering him if he made a mystery out of it himself. Didn't he expose his favorite theories to you yet? I see that he didn't really honor you with his confidence. He has less secrets with me. Anyway, he's a darling man and I adore him."

"Perhaps he was hiding some of his tastes because I inspired some others in him," said Michele spitefully.

She hated Felicia for having hidden this characteristic of her hero. Was it possible that she who knew everything didn't know about him?

" 'Lasciate ogni speranza, voi ch'entrate!' " said Diane. "Your esthetic is a man of principles: he doesn't allow himself to be swayed from his virtues and his ways."

"Oh, you know I've corrupted many others!" boasted Michele.

She was almost furious. Her aggressiveness was enchanting Diane, who amused herself by provoking Michele further.

"I'm afraid this one isn't corruptible."

"We'll see."

"Bravo! The woman who converts Gino will deserve a gold priapus. But if I were in your place, I wouldn't waste my time on such hopeless causes. There are so many better things to do. I'll tell you again that I know a hundred men as attractive as this one and who would be dying to give themselves to you. Do you want me to bring you some?"

"No," said Michele. "I like difficult victories."

"Alright, good luck!" concluded Diane jokingly.

She looked at Michele in the same way she had at the club.

"Have you been enjoying yourself lately?" she asked in a murmur.

"Yes," said Michele.

Diane looked at her a moment in silence.

"With whom?"

"I won't tell you."

"But you made love with someone, didn't you?"

"Yes."

Diane smiled at her in a friendly way.

"I've prepared something for you tonight if you like."

"What is it?" asked Michele, curious despite herself.

"I won't tell you."

Michele sulked. Diane allowed herself to give in:

"Two Parisians, who will only be here a day. I'll let you have them both all alone at first."

"And you?"

"Oh, you can leave a little for me!"

"Are you naked under your dress?"

"Yes."

"Show me."

This time, Michele was in too excited a state to resist. They had gradually moved away from the guests and were separated from them by a screen. She took the hem of her skirt and lifted it.

"Good," said Diane, her eyes riveted to the black, hairy pussy.

Michele felt her cunt softening under this examination as though it was being touched by fingers or a tongue. She held herself so that Diane's eyes could caress her.

"Show me more!" ordered Diane.

Michele obeyed, but her dress was still in the way.

"Lift it higher."

Michele nodded. She couldn't wait to be naked. Her nipples were demanding to be offered like her cunt. She lowered the shoulders and pulled on the zipper of her dress.

"Oh!" exclaimed Diane, "these damned intruders!"

The charm was broken. Michele felt as though she was coming out of a dream. She fixed her dress and shook her hair. Diane took her by the arm and led her further. A native boy appeared, carrying a tray. Both women drank some champagne in a single gulp.

Diane called the servant back and they exchanged their empty glasses for full ones. Michele was very thirsty. They no longer knew what to say to each other and were watching the people prattling loudly without really seeing them. It seemed to them that the temperature had gone up. Perhaps it was going to storm.

"Do you think it will storm?"

"Probably."

"It's so hot!"

"This dress is absurdly warm," thought Michele.

Someone waved to Diane and she seemed about to go away. Michele suddenly remembered what she wanted to ask her.

"Listen," she said, holding her back, "do you know an American girl with very short red hair? She's the sister of a naval attaché. She . . ."

"Fay?" interrupted Diane.

Michele felt her heart pounding. She would have found it normal if no one had known the foreigner and, although she wanted to find out about her she was upset at hearing her name on the Countess' lips, a contradiction which well illustrated the disorder of her thoughts at the moment.

"Yes," she admitted. "Is she here tonight?"

"She must be, but I haven't seen her."

"Why wouldn't she have come if she was invited?"

"I don't know."

"What kind of woman do you think she is?"

"How do you happen to know her?"

"I met her at Felicia's house."

"Oh, there's nothing surprising about that. She's one of her friends."

"Do you see her often?"

"Often enough."

"What does she do in Bangkok?"

"The same thing you and I do!"

"Why does her brother forbid her to do anything?"

"I don't think he forbids her. She has a lot of money. She doesn't need anyone."

The sentence resounded lugubriously in Michele's heart. She doesn't need anyone? She didn't doubt it.

She didn't know what else to ask. Without being able to explain herself, she didn't dare ask Fay's address.

"Well?" said Diane.

Michele knew what she was thinking, but she pretended she didn't. Diane continued:

"Are you coming tonight?"

"It's impossible—my husband."

"He'll trust you with me!"

But the temptation had passed. Diane was aware of it.

"Alright," she said. "I'll have them all to myself."

However, her good humor was false—she had lost her desire to indulge herself. Michele had a feeling that when the reception was over, Diane would go home to bed. The Countess said:

"There's your Gino! He looks like he's searching for someone. You, I'm sure! Don't let him languish."

She pushed Michele by the arm.

But the Italian had seen them himself and was walking toward them. The Countess said she was going to get something to drink. That was the last they saw of her.

"Felicia has told me a lot about you," he said.

"What could she have told you?"

"Enough to make me want to know you more. Will you dine with me soon so that we can talk? We can't converse here in this commotion."

"Thank you," said Michele. "But we have a guest at the house right now. It would be difficult . . ."

"Why? Leave him to your husband for one night. I hope you have permission to go out alone?"

"Of course," said Michele.

She wondered what David would think. She added, with some malice:

"But wouldn't you prefer that I bring my husband?"

"No," said Gino without the slightest ruffle. "The invitation is for you alone."

Michele was a little surprised. The style of this invitation did not match the reputation that Diane attributed to Gino. She would have liked to have cleared the matter up.

"It isn't proper for a married woman to dine with a gentleman alone," she said in a playful tone. "What do you think?"

"Proper?" said Gino as though he was hearing the word for the first time and found it difficult to pronounce. "Do you think it has to be proper? Is that one of your rules?"

"No, no!" Michele defended herself.

She tried a new tactic:

"But it's better for a woman to be warned in advance of the risk she is running."

"Everything depends on what you mean by risks. What is your conception of danger?"

Michele found herself on the witness stand again. Whether she referred to the duties of marriage, to the society's mores or to good morals, Gino's repost would be easy to predict. Besides, she had neither the courage nor the experience to express what she thought in the right words. All she could find to say was:

"I'm not afraid."

"I won't ask you anything else. Will you come tomorrow evening?"

"But I don't know where you live."

"Give me your address. I'll send a taxi for

you." He smiled charmingly. "I don't have a car."

"I could take mine."

"No, you'd get lost. The taxi will be at your house at eight o'clock. Is that convenient?"

"Yes."

She gave him her address.

Gino observed her silently and inscrutably. Finally he said:

"You're beautiful," simply and without emphasis.

"That's such a small thing," answered Michele politely.

CHAPTER FIVE

Gino seated his visitor on the soft red couch that was as smooth as satin. A native boy who was dressed only in tight blue shorts brought a tray of glasses and kneeled down to place it on the long, narrow coffee table.

Gino's house was made out of round logs. From the outside it looked like a forest cabin. This was in striking contrast with the luxury of the furniture and materials on the inside. The parlor opened onto the 'khlong.' From where she was sitting, Michele could see the fishing boats loaded with sweet drinks, coconuts, and bamboo filled with cooked rice as they crossed the islets of liana and leaves that were carried by the current. The man who was standing in the back leaning over the only oar was panting as he balanced himself and calmly looked into the room as he passed. The little copper bells in a nearby temple were sounding two notes, one shrill, the other sad and wounded. In the distance they could hear a gong calling the bonzes to bed and a woman's voice singing a lullaby to her child.

"A friend of mine is coming," said Gino.

His soft voice went well with the shadows of the buddhist statues that the laconic light from the lamps was tracing on the wall. Michele felt a kind of physical apprehension to the degree that she drank a very strong cocktail which the boy had served in one gulp. But the shock of the alcohol wasn't enough to undo the knot that was forming inside her. What was wrong with her, anyway? She was ashamed of this formless fear and she tried to break the absurd enchantment.

"Do I know him?" she asked.

It was only after she had spoken that the deception reached her. So, Gino didn't even want to be alone with her. She had thought he wanted to have her at his mercy. He hadn't accepted her husband and had decided to have someone else as a chaperon. Gino answered:

"No. I only met him yesterday at a party. He's English. An attractive person with a wonderful skin! The sun in this country has given him an even . . . how do you say it? . . . a color that smells good. You'll like him!"

Jealousy and humiliation were clawing at Michele's heart. Gino was talking about this man with a delight that suspended his sentence between each word, only seeming to make his choice after great thought. Michele imagined him, plate in hand, leaning over the glass case of a pastry assortment. What doubt could there be now about his tastes? Diane had been right to warn her! At the same time, however, Michele had the confusing impression that the merits of the expected guest were not only destined for the pleasure of the man who was describing them, but they were also destined for her.

Well, if Gino wanted to take her, she had nothing to say. She expected it. That was why she had come, resolved to please Felicia—or simply because the temptation was stronger than she wanted to recognize. The certitude of giving in caused her a pleasure as physical as that she would soon experience when she undid her dress, opened her legs, and felt a body she did not know till that moment touching her and his warmth entering her. Whether it would be in a single thrust or, on the contrary, slowly, inch by inch—leaving her waiting, opened, begging, uncertain and wet, in wonderful suspense! And to come again and again. How marvelous! So hard, so swollen, so stiff, caressing the inside of her cunt so imperiously, voluptuously, emptying itself to the last drop, leaving her fulfilled—hollowed clay, dug out, irrigated! She bit her lips. She was ready. She loved this possession of her body, she wanted it. But please let them spare her a complicated game: the idea tired her in advance. She would have to be suspicious of the Italian nature!

(She was on the verge of telling Gino: "You are right to profit by the opportunities that offer themselves, but be content with me as I am. Make love to me, then send me away so that I can sleep with my husband. When I have left, you'll be able to amuse yourself with your Englishman as you wish." But she imagined how she would feel if Gino looked at her with that expression of distant courtesy—of disdain—which she had already seen and answered: "My dear, you're mistaken. I like you very much, of course, but . . .")

Gino's voice, with the same tone that she attributed to him in her thoughts, interrupted these wanderings:

"I want you to show your legs as high as possible. Coleman will be sitting here. Will you turn a little so that your knees will be facing him and he can see through the shadows of your skirt?

Michele was dizzy. Gino had placed his hand on her naked shoulder, low enough so that the tips of his long fingers could press on her breast. He moved his hand slightly to the right while with the other hand he gently seized the sides of her black skirt and lifted the hem, uncovering her legs unequally: the left one to midthigh, the right even higher.

"No, don't cross them," he said. "That's perfect. And whatever you do, don't move. Here he is."

Gino took his hand away. She felt it sliding over her like a wave leaves the sand.

Gino seated the new guest, at the same time giving Michele a smile of encouragement like an examiner to a student who is frightened. But the Englishman seemed to be the most intimidated.

"He isn't even looking at my legs," thought Michele with less anger than vindictive joy at the defeat of Gino's machinations. Good for him! Suddenly Coleman seemed more of an ally than an enemy. She greeted him with a smile. It was true that he wasn't at all bad. And he certainly couldn't be a homosexual!

The new guest unfortunately didn't seem capable of speaking any French. "That's certainly my luck!" Michele observed ironically. "I must be fated to only fall in the hands of the big traveler who isn't gifted in languages." The word in French for 'language' which also meant 'tongue' secretly amused her and pricked her with a libertine arrow. She tried to imagine the sensations that Coleman's tongue would give her when it sought hers, then descended toward her cunt. She imagined it penetrating her, then caught herself and made a worthy effort to say several English phrases that she had learned during her three weeks in Bangkok, but this didn't help her. The man seemed delighted, nevertheless.

Gino obviously didn't wish to play interpreter. He mixed the drinks, giving his servant orders in a modulated idiom in which Michele did not recognize the inflections and resonances of the Siamese language which her ear was beginning to distinguish. Finally he came to sit on the floor in front of the sofa where Michele was sitting. He turned his back to her and faced his guest. They were speaking English. From time to time, the guest looked at Michele and tried to bring her into the conversation. Finally she decided that this treatment had lasted long enough.

"I don't understand," she said.

Gino lifted a surprised eyebrow and said:

"That doesn't matter."

Then before she had time to return the impertinence, he leaped to his feet, sat down next to her, put his arm around her waist, and, bending her back a little, cried to his visitor with an enthusiasm and warmth that left Michele stupefied:

"Non è bella, caro?"

He held her in that position which forced her to lift her legs and (she was conscious this time with a bit of amusement) to uncover them more. He ran his fingers over her lips then solemnly undid her dress. First he exposed one of her shoulders and her upper arm, then one nipple which he contemplated with rounded lips.

"She's really beautiful, don't you think?" he repeated.

The Englishman nodded. Gino recovered the breast.

"Do you like her legs?" he asked.

He had spoken the question in French and the guest blinked his eyes in response. Gino continued:

"They are *very* beautiful! They are special organs of eroticism."

He touched the line of the golden tibias with his fingers.

"It's perfectly clear that their function is not just walking."

He leaned over Michele.

"I would like you to give your legs to Coleman. Do you accept?"

She didn't understand what Gino meant and her head was spinning a little. But she didn't want to seem opposed to whatever he wanted.

She decided to remain impassive. He seemed satisfied.

He raised her skirt again but much higher this time. He had to lift Michele's body with his free arm because of the tightness of her skirt in order to completely display her legs and her lower abdomen. For the first time since her stay in Bangkok, Michele had put on stockings despite the heat. Her transparent black panties discreetly contained the silky curls and peeked through the diamond that her garterbelt made with the folds of her belly.

"Come here," said Gino. "Take them."

She saw the man moving toward her. First one then two hands caressed her ankles. Then one again, while the second rose along one calf then the other, pausing at her knees, at the beginning of her thighs, finally stopping there, as if impressed by all the space that lay beyond this final refuge of decency.

Then the other hand came to the rescue, joining the first to encircle her thighs, thin enough near the knees so that they could be almost completely enclosed in the fingers that were pressing them.

Then the hands progressed to the outside of the thighs and higher until they reached her buttocks. There they pushed her legs apart so that they could caress the inner surface, so sensitively that Michele felt her lips swelling.

Gino watched her. But she couldn't see him. When she opened her eyes and tried to read in his what was expected of her, he smiled in a way that made it impossible for her to decipher the meaning. Then as much out of spite as because she wanted to come, she lifted her skirt as high as possible, seized the elastic of her panties and lowered them. The Englishman's hands immediately became bolder and more helpful, and aided her in lowering her panties, pulling them over her legs to the ground.

Almost immediately Gino's voice, more serious and somber even than before, made Michele tremble. He was speaking English. After a few sentences, he translated for her:

"You shouldn't give everything to the same person," he said as though he were teaching her a difficult truth. Coleman has had your legs—he must be content with that for the moment. Keep the rest of your body for others on another occasion. One part of you to each man. You must give yourself in detail.

Michele didn't dare cry: "But what about you? What do you want? What part of my body tempts you?" She wondered with a sudden burst of derision, if all Gino needed was the breast he had caressed earlier. For a second, she hated him. But he quickly stood up, full of warmth and, clapping his hands, cried:

"How about dinner? Come, cara! I want you to taste the foods that drive the body wild."

He lifted her from the couch, sliding his arm under her shoulders, the other under her legs that were still uncovered and which seemed even longer from having been suspended. When he put Michele back on her feet, the black skirt fell into place. Michele leaned over with a graceful movement to pat it down. She saw a tiny spot of dark nylon on the floor and didn't know what to do. Gino picked it up with the tips of his fingers and pressed it against his lips.

" 'To break away from real things is nothing, but from memories!' " he said. " 'The heart breaks upon separation from dreams, there is so little reality in man!' "

Then he slid the perfumed garment into the chest pocket of his silk vest and, taking Michele by the hand, led her to the little round table which was surrounded by three seats of old wood with high backs in a quasi-medieval style.

Michele didn't dare look at Coleman. In spite of herself, she was amused by the strangeness of the experience and was beginning to forget her disappointment in Gino. She even thought that he had had some reason for having prevented her from giving herself to this beautiful stranger. She wasn't going to open her body to everyone who placed their hand on her knees, was she? It was already enough that she had done that on the plane. She had always known how to graciously discourage the boys. Obviously it wasn't the same with Gino. There was nothing unusual about a married woman sharing herself between her husband and her lover. And, now that Felicia had put the idea into her head, she really wanted to have a lover. But just one! And for this lover to be Gino! The thought suddenly came to her that perhaps he had wanted to keep her to himself. This hypothesis returned her good spirits.

However, she didn't want the Italian to know her true feelings so she tried to ridicule the dogmas and rituals of his philosophy, less because she attached any true importance to it than to show him that she wasn't so naive.

"I don't really see how your lovemaking by installments goes with the esthetic you professed to be last night. If it's necessary to be free and to live life fully, why are you telling me today to save myself and give myself sparingly?"

"Then give yourself all at once. What will happen when it's finished?" asked Gino.

"Finished?"

"Consider the woman who posed for the 'Portrait Ovale.' After she had given her ultimate color and had breathed her last breath, what art was possible? 'Finita la comedia!' When the last cry of pleasure has passed your lips, the work will be abolished. It will disappear like a dream. It will never have existed. Isn't the most imperious task in this mortal world, the only task when you weigh everything, to make things last? Of course it is! But not to finish them!"

"Are you trying to depict my approaching end too? You and your disciple, Felicia, really ought to come to some agreement. She keeps nagging me to use myself, you to economize. And both of you in the name of the brevity of life!"

"I see that you've misunderstood me, my dear! That's because I expressed myself poorly. Felicia was better at expressing what we both think. Little girls have a talent for explanations that we lose with age."

"No! Your lessons are completely contradictory. Yours teaches continence . . ."

"That's the most unjust reproach," Gino interrupted joyously. "But doesn't your indignation condemn you to abstinence?"

"What?"

"Your food is getting cold . . ."

Michele laughed a little sheepishly. Gino was too good at eluding embarrassing questions.

For a moment they talked about the foods and wines. Coleman only took a modest part in the conversation, although Gino flew from one language to the other. Michele sincerely praised the meal. She said that she ordinarily didn't attach too much importance to what she ate but that tonight even she found herself sensitive to the quality of the food.

"If gastronomy doesn't seem to be the most important thing in life, what does?" asked Gino.

Michele realized that the conversation was thereby authorized to ascend to the heights she had failed to reach during the hors d'oeuvres. She thought for a moment. What could she answer in order to keep up the tone of the conversation, without conceding too much? After all, she thought, the goal of this evening was clear: she had come here to give herself, not to philosophize. Therefore, she said in a natural voice:

"Making love."

Gino didn't seem appreciative. Instead he was impatient.

"No doubt, no doubt," he said. "But do you have to make love any way? Is it the orgasm that counts the most, or the manner of getting there?"

"The orgasm—without a doubt!"

She didn't really believe it. She was trying to provoke Gino. It appeared that she had only succeeded in astounding him.

"Dear God!" he sighed.

"Are you religious?" teased Michele.

"I'm invoking an esthetic god," he corrected. "A god whose laws you ought to know. I'm talking about Eros."

"Do you think I don't know how to serve him?" she rebuffed. "He's the god of love."

"No. He's the god of eroticism."

"Oh, is that what you've done to him!"

"Is a god ever anything else? You don't seem to me to have a very high idea of eroticism."

"You're wrong."

"Oh, really? And how do you conceive of it exactly?"

"Well, eroticism is . . . what shall I say . . . the cult of the pleasure of the senses, freed of all morals."

"Not at all," said Gino triumphantly. "It's exactly the contrary."

"It's the cult of chastity?"

"It isn't a cult, but a victory of reason over myth. It isn't a movement of the senses, it's an exercise of the mind. It isn't the excess of pleasure, but the pleasure of excess. It isn't a licence, it's a rule. And it's a moral code."

"Very pretty!" applauded Michele.

"I'm serious," said Gino. "Eroticism isn't a manual of recipes to enjoy yourself in society. It's a conception of the destiny of man, a gauge, a canon, a code, a ceremonial, an art, an instruction. It's also a science—or, rather, the fruit of choice, the final fruit of science. Its laws are based on reason, not on credulity. On confidence, not on fear. And on the enjoyment of life, rather than on the mystique of death."

Gino stopped the words that were on Michele's lips with a gesture and finished:

"Eroticism isn't a product of decadence, it's progress. Because it helps clarify sexual matters, it's an instrument of mental and social health. And I assert that it's an element of spiritual promotion, because it presupposes an education of character, the renouncement of the passions of illusion for the benefit of the passions of lucidity."

"Oh, that's wonderful," teased Michele. "Do you find this portrait tempting? Isn't it more agreeable to have illusions?"

"The madness of possession for you alone or of belonging to one person; the desire for power or servitude; the desire to cause suffering or to kill; the fascination, the desire, and the love of suffering and of death; and an appetite for eternity are those passions which I call illusions. Do they tempt you?"

"Not really," agreed Michele. "But tell me what should tempt me."

"I would like the supreme virtue to be a passion for beauty. That contains everything. What is beautiful is true, what is beautiful is justified, what is beautiful defies death. The love of beauty is what makes us rise above the animals. The miracle of beauty, which sprang from our rebellious curiosity and our pride, has been our escape. Beauty is the wing of the world—without beauty, the mind would be grounded."

Gino was silent an instant, but the expression on Michele's face encouraged him to continue.

"The beauty of science is what guards us from the disgrace of magic. And the beauty of reason makes us horrified at the deception of myths. Man will cure himself by finding the remedy to his dreams and nightmares in the continual advancement of his mind. There is no other need in life than intelligence, no other destiny than love, and no other sign of happiness than beauty."

He faced Michele and pointed an imperious finger at her.

"But remember, it isn't in the finished work that beauty awaits you. It isn't in success. Not the paradise promised to the loyal worker, nor the quietude of evening after the piety of work. It is the never-quiet creative blasphemy, the questions that nothing can satisfy, the march forward that never tires. It is defiance and it is effort."

Michele smiled and appeared to understand him, but he continued, as if he was especially anxious that his guest have no doubts about the ultimate object of his speech.

"Beauty wasn't given to man. He invented it. He makes it. Beauty isn't the order of nature, it is its opposite. It is the anxious hope of men against it, the virtue born of their solitude in the universe from which they chased the angels and devils, the promised victory over the weeds and rains. It is the imagined clarity of the moon, the song of sirens above the sea. Thus I say that eroticism, this triumph of dream over nature, is the high refuge of the spirit of poetry, because it repudiates the impossible. It is Man, who is capable of *everything.*"

"I don't understand this power too well," Michele objected.

"Love between women is a biological absurdity, it is impossible. Eroticism immediately makes a reality out of this dream, this invention. Sodomy is a defiance of nature: man does it. Making love with five people isn't *natural:* man imagines it, he orders it, and he accomplishes it. And each of these victories is *beautiful.* Certainly to expand this further, eroticism doesn't necessarily need these exceptions. It only demands the youth and liberty of the mind, love of the truth, a purity which owes nothing to customs and conventions. Eroticism is a passion for courage."

"To listen to you, one might think that this eroticism must be a kind of ascetic doctrine! Is it worth the pain to go through this?"

"A thousand times! Even if it were only for the pleasure of defying our monsters. And first the most hideous of all: ugliness and cowardice —the two cherished hydras of man! Men who never express themselves as well as in the cry of Hobbes, more true every day after three centuries: 'The sole passion of my life will have been fear!' Fear of being different. Fear of thinking. Fear of being happy. All these fears which are contrary to poetry and which have become the world's values: conformity, the respect for taboos and rites, hatred of imagination, the refusal for novelty, masochism, malevolence, envy, hypocrisy, meanness, lying, cruelty, and shame. In a word, evil! The true enemy of eroticism is the spirit of evilness."

"You're marvelous!" Michele cried. "And I believed that what some quite simply called vice, was actually eroticism."

"Vice, you say? What do you mean by that word? Vice means fault. Eroticism, neither more nor less than the other works of man, is not exempt from faults, errors, or relapses. But there is something which cannot exist. That is shame in eroticism. The qualities which the birth of an erotic act demand: logic and firmness above all; imagination, humor, audacity, not to mention the power of one's convictions and talent for organization, good taste, esthetic intuition, and a sense of grandeur without which all his endeavors would be useless, can only make something proud, generous, and triumphant of a man."

"Is that why you speak of it as a moral code?"

"No, it's because of much more than that. Eroticism demands a systematic mind above all. Its followers can only be people with principles—theorists: not joyous playboys announcing their conquests."

"Then eroticism is the opposite of making love?"

"That's going too far. But it's true that making love isn't necessarily committing an act of eroticism. There is no eroticism where there is the sexual pleasure of compulsion, habit, or duty; where there is a pure and simple response to a biological instinct, a physical intent rather than esthetic intent, a search for pleasure of the senses rather than pleasure of the mind, love of oneself or love of others rather than love of beauty. In other words, there is no eroticism where there is *nature*. Eroticism like all morals is man's effort to oppose, surmount, and surpass nature. You know very well that man is only man to the extent that he makes a denatured animal of himself and that he only becomes better when he separates himself more from nature. Eroticism, the most human talent of men, is not the opposite of love, it's the opposite of nature."

"Like art?"

"Bravo! Morality and Art are as one. I'm overjoyed to hear you speak of art as of antinature. Haven't I already told you that beauty only reveals itself in the defeat of nature? From age to age those who cast shadows on the sea of our lives try to convince humanity, most often by stomping on it, that it can only cure itself of the fatigue of machines and architectures by a 'return to nature.' What a sickening panic! What an abominable forfeiture of intelligence!"

He paced back and forth for a moment and then continued excitedly:

"I don't believe that man has come so far from so low a position to stop here. He'll continue! What we are capable of is trying to add to our intelligence and do the impossible to be happy."

"And is eroticism capable of helping us discover a new world?" asked Michele.

"More than that: it is progress itself."

"But since the erotic man of the future hasn't appeared yet, the erotic age you dream of is only a vision of the future. You and I haven't a chance! We were born too soon!"

"Who can say?" said Gino. "The laws of evolution are still hidden to us. Perhaps we aren't born yet."

"What can we do to be born?" cried Michele.

"Act as if you are master of life. Act as if you are alive! Practice eroticism as a rule of life. This could be the decisive step to pass from the age of fear to the age of reason."

He sighed.

"Oh, certainly we would prefer to have been born a million years from now! But let's do our best to bring the age of reason closer to us. As for me, I know what my duty is: to shout to the world that the body is good, that its powers are infinite, that the sweetness of life is also the 'raison d'etre' of life."

Gino continued to expand his various theories of eroticism for an hour. He advanced his belief that the ultimate pleasure for a woman is to have two lovers at the same time. Michele was surprised and tried to joke about this theory.

"In other words, when my husband wants to make love to me I should say: Impossible, there's just the two of us here!"

Gino did not laugh and quickly countered with:

"Why did you get married?"

Michele didn't know what to answer. She had the impression that someone had just taken her by the shoulders and was turning her around so that she would lose her balance. She felt as though her eyes were covered, her arms held out, and she didn't dare move for fear of falling. She didn't want to admit to Gino that she had married David because she loved him—or even for the pleasure of making love with him. Fortunately, an idea came to her that she thought would change the subject.

"I'm a lesbian," she said.

Gino's eyelashes fluttered imperceptibly.

"Good," he announced.

Then, suspiciously:

"But have you always been—or were you just during your childhood?"

"Always," said Michele.

But a wave of distress came over her which she hadn't expected. Was she telling the truth? Would she ever be able to take a female body in her arms? In losing Fay, hadn't she lost everything . . .

"Does your husband know your tastes?"

"Naturally. Everyone knows them. It's not a secret. I'm proud that I love pretty girls and that they love me."

Gino got up and walked around the room. He seemed transported. He came back and took Michele's hand, kneeling at her feet. To her surprise, he kissed her knees lightly, then put his arms around her legs.

" 'Women are all beautiful," he murmured, with a fervor in his deep voice. " 'Women alone know how to love.' "

Michele thought then, with an ironic melancholy, that she had no luck at all. It was just like her to be in love at the same time with a woman who wasn't homosexual enough and a man who was too much!

He had recovered his nonchalance and was continuing his interrogation.

"Have you had many women?"

"Yes."

She told herself that she wouldn't let the memory of Fay spoil this evening. She said:

"I like to change them often."

"Do you find as many as you like?"

"It isn't difficult. I only have to ask them."

"Aren't there any who refuse?"

"Very few!" minimized Michele. "Of course," she corrected with a happy laugh, "there are some girls who aren't corruptible. But that's too bad for them!"

"Exactly!" said Gino. "And you? Are you easy to conquer?"

She smiled and said:

"On the condition that they are really pretty. I have a hatred of every girl who isn't beautiful."

"Excellent," complimented Gino again. "Your husband, you tell me, knows about your feminine affairs. But does he approve of them?"

"He even encourages them. I've never had so many girls as I have since I got married."

"Isn't he afraid that their caresses will turn you from him?"

"What an idea! Making love with a woman is quite different from making love with a man. One doesn't replace the other. You need both. It's as terrible to be purely a lesbian as it is not to be one at all."

"I presume that your husband profits from your mistress' charms himself?" he asked.

Michele smiled:

"There are some who only dream of that."

"Aren't you jealous?"

"That would be ridiculous!"

"You're right. Sharing would only add to your pleasure."

Michele thought of the naked bodies of her lovers, so naked, so soft to touch, so beautiful! She scarcely heard Gino's final comment.

"And what about him?" he asked after a moment of silence.

Michele opened her eyes.

"Him?"

"Yes, your husband. Do you get many men for him?"

"What?" she said, truly shocked. "No!"

She felt herself blushing.

"Not even since your marriage?" pursued Gino.

She couldn't prevent herself from an expression of indignation.

"In that case," declared Gino icily, "I don't understand what reason there is to be married."

He took a sip of his drink and continued in a disdainful tone.

"Does he forbid you to make love to other men?"

Michele answered quickly.

"No, not at all." But down deep in her heart, she wasn't really sure.

"Has he told you that you could?"

"Not exactly, of course. But he has never forbidden me. And he doesn't ask me whether I do or not. He leaves me free."

"Then you ought to reproach him. Eroticism doesn't need this liberty."

Michele tried to understand what Gino meant.

"When you were alone in Paris and were writing to your husband, did you tell him about your lovers?"

Michele was crushed by the awareness of her banality. She shook her head, then cried to elude the question:

"I told him about my women!"

Gino wiped them away with a gesture and they were both quiet again. Michele looked at Coleman. He was smiling. She wondered if he truly understood what they were saying or if this smile was simply to hide that fact that he was bored.

"But I don't think that David would be jealous," she said trying to erase the bad impression that she had produced on Gino. "He is no more jealous than I am. Wait, he's the one who taught me to show my legs. And I wear tight dresses to give him pleasure so that when I get out of a car my skirt hikes up as much as possible. And you can see that even in the most conventional situation, I sit very immodestly."

She laughed.

"You see that this doesn't shock me. Isn't it a proof that we are both disposed to eroticism?"

"Yes."

"He's also the one who determines the necklines of my dresses. Do you know many husbands who uncover their wife's breasts as generously?"

"Do *you* find it agreeable to show your breasts?"

"Yes," said Michele. "But especially since David taught me. Before I knew him, I liked to be touched, I mean by girls, but I didn't care about being seen or not. I didn't get any pleasure out of it. Now I do."

She added bravely:

"I wasn't born an exhibitionist. I became one! Thanks to him." And she repeated: "You see!"

"Have you ever asked yourself why your husband liked showing you off in public so much?" asked Gino. "If it's only to make a vamp out of you, it's scarcely laudible. And if it's out of simple pride, to parade his wife's beauty like richness, that's hardly any better."

"Oh, no!" protested Michele, who couldn't stand to hear her husband talked about like that. "That's not at all like him. If he makes me show my body, it's rather to make others profit by it . . ."

"Then that's just what I told you!" triumphed Gino. "If your husband tries to make you awaken the desires of men, if he offers you in this way to them, it's because he wants you to make love with them."

"But . . ." Michele tried to object.

This idea had never occurred to her and she could find nothing to help her refute it. However she was speechless at first. Was it possible that David expected that of her?

Finally she pleaded:

"But why would David want me to deceive him? What sort of pleasure could a man get from others possessing his wife?"

"Let's see," said Gino, and his voice was severe. "Can you tell me that you don't understand how an evolved man could want his wife to seduce other men? Be logical: if your husband likes to know that you make love with women, why should he think differently of men? Is there really a distinction in nature as essential as you seem to believe between hetero and homosexual love? I think that there is only one love, and that making it with men or women, with husbands, lovers, brothers, sisters, or children is all the same."

"But David has always known that I loved girls, even before he deflowered me. I told him the first day I met him."

And she added quickly:

"And naturally, if I had had a brother, I would have made love to him. But I'm an only child!"

"So?"

"So? . . . So, I mean that by caressing a woman, I'm not deceiving my husband!"

Her host appeared amused.

"Does he make love to men?"

"No!" Michele found the idea of her husband being a homosexual absurd.

"You're not fair," observed Gino, who had guessed her thoughts.

"It's not the same!"

Gino smiled and she was no longer sure . . .

"Would you prefer him to sleep with other women?"

"I don't know . . . I suppose so."

"Then," he cried triumphantly, "why wouldn't he think of you in the same way?"

"That's true," she admitted.

"Another example!" pursued Gino without

waiting for a response. "Do you expose your legs and breasts out of simple habit or because it excites you to offer yourself?"

"Naturally it excites me!"

"Physically?"

"Yes."

"Is your pleasure greater if your husband is present?"

She reflected: "I think so."

"When you're sitting next to him and a man is trying to look under your dress, don't you sometimes dream that he would slide his hands under you, not to mention the rest?"

"Of course," she admitted laughingly.

But this didn't convince her that David could enjoy imagining the same scene. Gino sighed.

"You still have much to learn. You still are not aware of what separates the simple sexuality from the erotic art."

Then he continued, adding a note of irony to the word Michele had utilized:

"If your husband didn't want you to 'deceive' him, why would he have let you come here alone tonight? Did he object?"

"No. But perhaps he thought that dining with a man doesn't necessarily mean that I'm going to give myself to him."

Michele acted natural. She didn't know if her point had been taken or not. Gino appeared lost in meditation. Just when she was beginning to let her own thoughts wander, he asked:

"Are you ready to give yourself tonight, Michele?"

It was the first time he had called her by her name. She did her best to hold back the emotion that she experienced in hearing this question asked so negligently. She tried to give her voice the same uninvolved tone in order to prove her liberty:

"Yes."

"Why?"

She was immediately embarrassed again.

"Do you give in to men easily?" asked Gino.

She felt ashamed. Couldn't he see that this conversation was mortifying her? She felt the need to say:

"It's quite the contrary," with a vehemence which was not customary for her. "I told you that I had many women lovers. I didn't tell you that I had many men. To tell the truth," she added, moved by a sudden impulsion (and because she didn't like to lie and did it as seldom as possible), I've never had one. Now, you understand why I had nothing to tell my husband —until now," she finished with a smile that was difficult to interpret.

At the same time as she admitted to this virtue, she thought that in truth she was not really lying. Could anyone seriously call the strangers who had possessed her on the plane lovers? Felicia had agreed that they didn't count. And she had gradually come to doubt the reality of that adventure and to consider that in giving in to that sort of awake-dream which she had had between heaven and earth, she had not been more unfaithful than in enjoying the imaginary embraces of other men while her husband came in her body each night.

For the first time, she thought that perhaps she was pregnant from one of the travelers.

She would soon know. But that was of little importance.

Gino, however, seemed to experience an increased interest in his guest.

"Are you making fun of me? I thought I heard you say that you 'also' like men?"

"Why yes. Aren't I married? And I just told you that I'm ready to give myself to another man besides my husband, even tonight."

"Then for the first time?"

Michele nodded her head in a half-lie.

(Provided, she thought with sudden anguish, that Felicia hadn't given away her secret! But no, it was clear that Gino knew nothing.)

"Perhaps I was ready for it on other occasions, but no one has profited from it yet," she added.

He attacked quickly:

"Why do you want to deceive your husband? Is it because he leaves you unsatisfied physically?"

"Oh, no!" cried Michele overwhelmed and suddenly unhappy. "Oh, no! He's a marvelous lover! I'm not at all dissatisfied, I assure you. It's not because of that, on the contrary . . ."

"Ah!" said Gino, " 'on the contrary?' That's interesting. Could you tell me what you mean by this 'on the contrary'?"

She was furious at him. He had just demonstrated that David himself wanted her to have lovers and he didn't seem to remember it . . .

But why in fact, she wondered, had she accepted the idea of being unfaithful so easily today? Why had she for the first time in her life and so suddenly so much desire to be a married woman who has a lover? Because that's exactly what she wanted: to be an *adulteress.* She wanted it—without loving David with less passion, however—*on the contrary!* What had happened to her? Before she had time to reflect on the meaning of her words, she heard herself say:

"It's because I'm happy. It's . . . it's because *I love him!*"

Gino leaned over her.

"In other words, if you want to deceive your husband, it's not because he bores you, or from weakness, or to avenge yourself, but, on the contrary, it's because he makes you happy. It's because he taught you to love what is beautiful. To love the marvels of physical pleasure given by the penetration of a man's body deeply in yours. He taught you that love is the overwhelming of the senses—that moment when a man's nudity crushes yours. That what gives endless splendor is that movement of your hands to your shoulders to lower your dress to the waist and uncover your breasts, and that movement of your hands to your hips to lower your dress to your feet and make you a more adorable statue than you already are. He taught you that beauty is not the solitude of your body, but its expansion. That beauty is not to wait for other hands to undress you, but the haste and the simplicity of your fingers liberating you themselves and holding you out like a tribute to the body to whom you are destined. He has taught you that there is no other beauty, that there is no other happiness. That this desired passion of your body, this organization of your powers, was the bearer of an infinite intelligence—that only the endlessness of repetition could accomplish. And that no other act of conscience made more sense than the reflected quest and the knowing embrace of a single instant—of that lucid second in which the woman makes herself the man's harvest and his feast."

Michele listened, not knowing whether she should let herself be enveloped by the rambling of his words, and let them decide what she was, or . . . She handed Gino her glass that was sparkling with reflections, and raised her eyes to him.

"Is that the way you will give yourself?" he asked.

She lowered her head.

"And you'll tell your master that he can be proud of you?"

She lost her serenity and let out a cry of alarm:

"Oh, no!"

Then, after a hesitation:

"Not immediately . . ."

Gino looked at her indulgently.

"I see," he said. "But you have to learn."

"What do I have to learn?" she protested.

"The pleasure of relating your affairs. More subtle, more refined even than the secret itself. The day will come when even the savor of your adventures will be less to you than the passion of reciting them in detail to someone who is the most attentive of your spectators. But there's no hurry and if, for the moment, hiding it is easier for you, keep your husband in ignorance of the progress of his student. Anyway, perhaps it's preferable for you to wait until your progress is completely conclusive. The surprise for him will be even better. But you'll need another guide during this time, if it isn't he, because the ways of eroticism are often abrupt and you might get discouraged or be led astray by yourself. What do you think?"

Michele judged that the question was rhetorical and decided it would be better to remain silent. Gino continued:

"But you know that following a disciple must be without limits. No guide in the world can be the substitute for your own will. He can show you the way, but you must walk it alone, knowing where your steps will lead you. The initiation into any art is a time of labor more than pleasure. One day the memory of your hard work will be sweet to you. Today you must decide freely. Are you ready to try anything?"

"Anything?" she asked.

She remembered that these had been Felicia's words a few days earlier.

"That's right. Anything!" said Gino.

Michele tried to imagine what 'anything' could be—and only succeeded in imagining the abandonment of her body to Gino. Since she had decided to give herself to him anyway, did the manner in which he took her have much importance? She even thought, with a little irony, that her mentor might be exaggerating the virtues of his amorous methods or thinking that the experience he had in store for her would change her. She wasn't that accustomed to men, but she was convinced that a woman had to do more to become capable of progress than just submit to the singularities of a lover. This amused her but not enough for her to want to discourage him.

What troubled her, however, was not being able to explain why, despite Gino's assurances, she preferred that this liaison remain unknown to her husband. It wasn't really out of the fear that Gino was mistaken about David's motives, she reflected. It was more for the reason that she had suspected earlier and which she hadn't known how to express. 'Deceiving' a husband that one loves was a special pleasure, which she had not thought of until now, but the temptation of which was making her temples beat with impatience. It was very possible, she thought, that, in the world of eroticism, the husband's complicity, the confession of the adulteress, constituted a more advanced freedom. But she wasn't there yet. The secret of her affairs was capable, in her eyes, of adding more than detracting from the pleasure she expected. Before learning the complicated art whose rules Gino had been discussing, she wanted to be happy with her simple desires. Isn't the adulteress already offering herself marvelous discoveries?

In reality, without her knowledge, an abstract eroticism was inspiring her more than the elementary sexuality to which she imagined she was giving herself, because it was less the anticipation of the pleasures that her lover would give her that was pushing her to abandon herself and was already exciting her, than the desire to deceive David, to deceive him as much as she loved him, to deceive him quickly, with her whole body, with all her nudity, with all the softness of her belly on which the stranger's semen would flow.

Gino was watching her and his eyes disturbed her. She changed positions on the couch, showing her legs as she had explained she knew how to do. She thought that Gino had spoken to her about making love with two men because he wanted to share her with his friend. "All right!" she said to herself. "I'll learn." She would have preferred to just have an affair with Gino or, if there were no way of avoiding Coleman, for him just to be a spectator. But she was determined not to oppose any of her host's demands. Perhaps, she recognized, she also wanted to be possessed by Coleman? And since Gino said that love with two men was so wonderful . . .

"Have you already at least made love with several women?" asked her hero.

She was amazed again that he could read her thoughts so easily. He must know how much she desired him. He was looking at her legs. She forgot to answer. She was happy that he was sensitive to her body. But he did not allow himself to be so easily distracted from his curiosity. He continued:

"I mean, with several women at the same time."

"Yes," said Michele.

He appeared charmed.

"Well," he said. "You're not so innocent!"

"But why would I be?" she asked. "I never pretended that I was."

The suspicion of good morals had become the worst insult that anyone could give her. If showing her legs wasn't enough, she was going to get right up on the couch and undress. The impulse was so strong that she curled her legs under her and got on her knees. And if this demonstration didn't conquer her host, she would masturbate in front of him! Her breasts were burning; perhaps it was Gino's liquor that was giving her such sudden audacity. But the Italian remained nonchalant. He seemed more anxious for verbal eroticism than for action. He pursued his inquest.

"And what do you do when you're exchanging caresses with two girls at the same time?"

Michele was impatient. To hasten the end of this conversation, she described scenes in which her imagination took over where realism left off. She didn't want to search her mind for details of her memories. A grain of invention, she thought, would please Gino more than a faithful history. He was not fooled by it.

"That all seems like the games of a young girl," he said. "It's time to grow up, my pretty friend."

Vexed, she tried to avenge herself. When she realized that, in letting an inopportune allusion escape, she would risk destroying his own plans, she tried to hold her tongue, but it was too late.

"And what about you," she said, "are you better with boys?"

To her surprise, however, Gino didn't seem at all embarrassed. On the contrary, his voice was filled with good humor.

"We're going to show you that, dear!"

He said something to Coleman in English. Michele wondered if the two men were going to give her an on-the-spot demonstration.

CHAPTER SIX

Michele thought she must be dreaming. The new place she was discovering hardly resembled the streets bordered by concrete houses or the villas hidden in the greenness of their gardens which she had known since her arrival in Bangkok. The full moon lended a paleness and animated relief to the decor which went all too well with the kind of ballet she had to execute in her movements. Decor is really the word with all that it evokes of fake perspectives, stages, cardboard walls, unstable platforms. Following Gino and followed by Coleman, she was apprehensively placing her high heels one after another on a gangway made out of a plank about thirty feet long and a foot wide that was thrown between two boards that were being licked by the thick, immobile waters of a canal which seemed to be a sewer. The weight of the walkers inflected the wood and made it bounce like a diving-board. Michele had no doubt that sooner or later she would be thrown into the slime.

When they reached the board, they had to walk over the plank that followed and which seemed even more shaky and worm-eaten than the one they had just left. This is what the trio did for several hundred feet with nothing at all to indicate that this strange path was close to its end. As she moved, Michele had the impression that she was going farther and farther away from the known world. Even the air that she was breathing had a different consistency and a strange odor. The night offered so total a silence that she tried not to breathe or talk as though it would have been a sacrilege. Suddenly she became aware that the silence was, in reality, made up of the uniform, uninterrupted, and strident cries of the crickets.

Michele and her guides had left the house a half-hour earlier on a narrow boat which had come to float along Gino's dock upon his call. They had climbed the 'khlong' and then later left the small boat for this wooden sidewalk which was oriented perpendicularly to the axis of the big canal, which must have been very shallow since even the light Siamese canoes were unable to go into it.

The canal was bordered from place to place by low huts with walls of rust-colored iron or blackened bamboo.

All the doors and windows were carefully barricaded as if closed against the plague. Michele wondered how the people breathed. She could understand the mode of life of those who lived in the 'sampans' and which they had passed earlier along the canal's banks. Profiting from the rainless night, men, women, and children had been sleeping outside under the stars. Their bodies were squeezed together and many of them had their eyes open. But what mystery cloistered these people, pushing them to protect themselves from the slightest breath of air in these clammy prisons?

The fantastic atmosphere was accentuated the farther they went. It seemed scarcely believable that this unsociable street of putrid water and dead wood where one moved by walking on a tightrope could last so long and lead nowhere. And when the riverside came out of its den in the daylight, how would they cross over this sole way of access to their territory? Michele already feared the acrobatics it would take if by accident other night prowlers met their group. To tell the truth, she doubted that it would happen because the country into which her companions were leading her was too lunar for living beings to have a chance to appear there.

However the very next minute a man surged out of the cottages. He was very tall with a muscular body the color of coals. A piece of red material covered his lower torso. He removed it pensively, watching the three people approaching. Now he was entirely naked. He then urinated in the water. Michele had never seen a virile member at rest which was as long as his, even in her imagination. Flaccid like that, it was as large as her husband's was erect. It's beautiful! she thought. And the man was completely beautiful. When they drew closer he watched them from less than a few feet. She was only thinking of one thing: that cock. What if it stood up . . . But the Siamese man remained cool. He looked at Michele's half-naked breasts and his member did not budge. The funambulists passed and went away.

They came to a crossing. The ghost-like path divided. Gino hesitated. He consulted Coleman, and finally chose one of the branches. Michele was afraid that it would not be the right one because they had been walking such a long time. But she didn't dare say anything. She had not uttered a word since they had left the boat. Suddenly, however, a cry escaped her lips. The road had made a turn and suddenly led into a sort of court (Michele had thought: a clearing, she was so tempted to believe that she was lost in a jungle!). Facing them about eighty feet away, a silhouette was looming into sight which she had seen in the distance above the roofs, but had taken for a tree. A little closer it seemed to be Genghis Khan, thick moustache, merciless eyes, daggers around his waist and hands on the daggers, muscles flexing, and bathed in moonlight. Michele's heart was pounding. No doubt this was the beginning of some sorcery. In an instant, grimacing Mongols were going to jump out to watch them. Michele would be given up to the rites of a murderous magic. At the same time as her imagination, more rapid than her reasoning, built a world of phantoms, a nervous laugh attested that she had not lost all her self-control. Leaning against the conqueror was a ballerina in a tutu who looked like a toy next to the giant and was smiling up at the stars.

Other people in multi-colored cardboard were thrown about, some standing, the rest thrown down.

"That makes a bizarre sight, all those moving props in such a place," she observed so that the sound of her voice would reassure her. "I wonder how they could get them here. Is there another means of access besides this bridge?"

(She suspected that her guide had inflicted a useless test on her.)

"No," said Gino.

He didn't feel the need to add any other commentary.

They went through the placard depot, passing between the great khan's legs, going around a palisade of steel, finding themselves in a little court again, where a half-opened door stood with a yellow light peeking through. Gino stopped on the threshold, shouted something, then went in without waiting for an answer. Michele felt less and less calm. The place was hostile. There was an odor that was difficult to define. Something like a mixture of dust, smoke, tea, and licorice. In the windowless room they entered, a bench covered with a torn cretonne was the only furniture. A dirty curtain in a terrible blue color obstructed the back. Almost immediately it was parted by a hand and a woman appeared.

The sight of her calmed Michele a little. She was an old Chinese woman (she must have been at least a hundred years old, Michele thought), whose perfect oval face was so wrinkled that it looked like a veil. Her complexion was like old ivory, almost turned orange. The white shiny hair was carefully pulled back and tied in a chignon. Her eyes and lips were so thin that you could scarcely make them out through the folds in her skin. It was only when the old woman began to speak, uncovering her teeth which were lacquered with black, that Michele closed her mouth.

The woman's hands were hidden in the pockets of her stiff tunic, which the shiny silk of the huge black pants made to appear even whiter by contrast.

Having finished a long speech to which Gino had not seemed to pay any attention, the hostess bowed with a suppleness that was surprising because it was so tempting to think that she was made of dead wood. Then she pivoted and disappeared into the bowels of the hut. They followed her without saying a word. The hut that they went through was perfectly dark at first. Michele had the impression that the shadows were dying there. She was really afraid. They went into a very small room where she discovered unhappily that two very old and almost musty men were stretched out completely naked on a wood partition. Their eyes were blinking and she had time to notice their large and dreamy pupils which didn't seem to see her. She had hastily caught a glimpse of their wrinkled cocks and dry testicles but the group was already moving into another room that was very similar to the preceding one except that it was not occupied. The old Chinese woman stopped. So this was where she had been leading them! She made a new sermon then disappeared as if through a trapdoor.

"What's happening?" asked Michele. "What

was she talking about? And what are we doing in this den? Everything is so disgusting!"

"It's only in your mind, said Gino. "This is dilapidated, but tidy."

Another woman appeared who was much younger than the first but much uglier. She was carrying a round tray with an alcohol lamp on it and an elongated glass on top of it. It was about an inch thick. Also on the tray were tiny little round tin boxes, long steel needles as large as those used to darn stockings, dried palm leaves cut in rectangles, and an instrument which Michele could not identify at first: a brown bamboo tube approximately the length of an arm and about as thick as a flute. At first sight, it seemed that the tube was closed on both ends, but she noticed that one of them was in reality pierced by a hole the size of a match. Rosy designs were incrusted along its length. On two-thirds of it, from the perforated extremity, was a sort of wood polyhedron, so shiny that the flames from the lamp were dancing in it and changing colors. At the end was what seemed to be a bowl, very small, very flat, no thicker than Michele's wrist, and balanced on the tube to which it was only held by a narrow point of contact. Its exterior surface was sunk in in its center by a cavity the size of a pearl on the bottom of which you could make out a very tiny orifice.

Gino anticipated his student's question.

"What you're looking at, my dear, is an opium pipe. Isn't it a beautiful object?"

"A pipe!" she said. "It doesn't look like one. Where do you put the tobacco? In that ridiculous little hole? It must be used up very quickly."

"You don't put tobacco in it. You put in a pellet of opium. And you only take a single puff. Then you fill it up again. But it's better if you see for yourself."

"You don't intend to make me smoke that drug, do you?"

"Why not? I want you to know what this game—or this art—consists of. You must know about everything."

"And . . . what if I like it?"

"What would be wrong with that?" Gino laughed.

"Relax. I didn't bring you here to addict you to opium. It will only be a prelude."

"And then what will happen?"

"You'll know in time. Don't be impatient, *cara*. The opium ceremony requires a perfect equanimity."

Michele did a complete about-face.

"Can I come back if I like it?"

"Certainly," said Gino.

Michele's questions seemed to amuse him. He contemplated her indulgently, almost with tenderness in his eyes.

"I thought it was illegal to smoke opium," she said.

"Of course. And also to make love outside of marriage."

"What would we do if the police came?"

"We would go to prison." Gino made a face and added: "But not without first having tried to buy the police with your charms."

Michele smiled skeptically. She teased:

"But since I'm married, I'm only negotiable at the price of another crime."

"You and the representatives of the law would commit that crime with the help of God."

He repeated the gesture he had made at his house, uncovering one of Michele's shoulders and breast. And, holding that breast in his hand, he asked:

"Isn't that so?"

Michele's face expressed doubt but also contentment, because she was happy that Gino was undressing her and touching her.

"Wouldn't you agree to give this service to us?" he asked.

She assured him:

"Yes. You know very well . . ." Then, with hesitation: "And . . . the policemen, how many would there be to operate that kind of raid?"

"Oh, not more than twenty."

She laughed again.

The servant had placed her tray in the center of the partition. Gino let go of Michele's breast (which she left uncovered), put his arm around her waist, and made her take a step forward.

"Stretch out here," he said.

"Me? But is it clean? It looks very hard."

"Why would the establishment need the expense of a mattress when this smoke is enough to soften anything, to make the hardest bed soft? Don't complain about the cleanliness, a mattress would be washed less easily than wood. Let that thought appease your worries."

Michele sat down with repugnance on the extreme edge of the platform, while her two companions stretched out on either side of her, so that the three made a circle around the lamp. After a few minutes she triumphed over her disgust and imitated them, leaning on her elbow, her head in the palm of her hand. She couldn't take her eyes off the oblong flame which was rising steadily from the interior of the thick glass tube. It was fascinating.

The Chinese woman was kneeling at the foot of the plank and had opened one of the little boxes. It was filled with a dark, opaque, almost solid honey. The woman scooped up a drop on the tip of one of the long needles that was as thick as a grain of wheat. She held it over the lamp a minute, rolled it on one of the fragments of fibrous leaves which she held in her other hand, then exposed it to the flame again. The burned drop crackled, puffed up, doubled in size, turning beautiful colors and became so pure and so brilliant that the neighboring objects were mirrored in it. It was abounding with life.

"It's beautiful," murmured Michele.

She was thinking that this spectacle alone was well worth the trip. "I'll never get tired of watching that little ball. It's like a precious stone that's trying to say something. But no stone is as beautiful."

Twenty policemen, she remembered. That's a lot. But to save Gino from prison, she would surely do anything.

She felt sorry when the woman who had finally given the drop of opium the form of a tiny translucid cylinder, exactly proportioned to the cavity of the pipe, introduced it quickly and pulled the needle away. Without losing a moment's time, she turned the pipe around, with the chamber down over the lamp, almost touching the orifice of the burning glass. She held out the opening to Gino who applied it to his lips and breathed in. The flame rose, burning the amber pearl. Gino's breath which was pulling up the mysterious smoke, seemed inexhaustible to Michele.

"Your turn," he said. "Don't let the smoke come out of your nose, don't choke, don't cough, breathe slowly and continuously."

"I'll never be able to!"

"That doesn't matter. Try."

The acolyte prepared another pipe. Again the brown sun flamed at the end of the magical wand, swelling and panting as if with desire. Michele saw an image of her cunt, calling with its swollen lips to the fire's ram that would pierce it, leave it bruised, burned, and satiated. It was pleasant, she thought, to feel her cunt becoming more wet as the little glistening drop became filled with passion above the flame. She liked this rite as if by following it she was publicly, ceremonially preparing herself to make love. She held her naked breast in her hand. She was happy. The tableau only needed one thing to be perfect: for the assistant to be a young sweet beautiful girl with an innocent face and an offered body which Gino, Coleman, and she would undress by degrees and with whom they would play together or by turns, each according to his desires and to the extremes of his pleasure. What a shame that her mentor hadn't foreseen that! She was on the point of reproaching him for it but she didn't dare. For a second, however, she had such a desire for a girl's legs to be entwined with hers and for a girl's pussy in which she could put her fingers that the Chinese girl almost looked beautiful to her.

When the pipe was held out to her, she let the opium burn without breathing it. The flame went out immediately. The woman had to pierce the reddish pearl with her needle again. At the second try, Michele succeeded in absorbing a little smoke. She laughed out loud.

"I like the taste," she said, "and the odor even more. It's a little like caramel. But it hurts my throat."

"You have to drink some tea."

Gino gave the servant an order. She got up and immediately came back with some very small wide cups without handles and a liliputian teapot that was filled to the brim with green tea. She filled it with boiling water, and immediately spilled the contents into a cup. The mixture had already taken on a copper color. The perfume that was coming from it was penetrating. It was more like that of jasmine than of tea. Michele burned her tongue and let out a cry.

"You have to take in a breath of air at the same time as you drink to cool your tea," said Gino. "Or, more exactly, to be able to drink it boiling hot without it hurting you. Like this."

He made a gargling noise.

"But that's the most impolite of all!" said the indignant student.

"In China, it's polite."

Now Coleman was drawing on the pipe. He wasn't as successful as his friend.

"I want to try again," said Michele impatiently, very excited by the novelty of the experience. "What am I going to dream about?"

"Nothing. First of all, opium doesn't make you dream. It makes you lucid and relieves you of physical misery and mental fetters. Secondly, before feeling whatever effect you might, you need to smoke several pipes."

"Well, then I'm going to smoke them!"

"You'll have just one more, that's all. If you went beyond that tonight, the only pleasure you would get would be my holding your head while your stomach turned inside out."

Michele wasn't too disappointed by this because the new pipe cost her a bout of coughing and she didn't find it as good as the first. As for Gino and Coleman, neither of them accepted even the second experience.

"Are you so afraid of getting intoxicated?" said their companion.

"My dear," retorted Gino, "I'm going to tell you a very big secret. It's that opium, taken in excess, takes a good part of one's male passion away. And we didn't come here, as you know, for the pleasures of the mind, but for those of the body."

"Oh, yes!" said Michele, again ill at ease. She found that this shabby place did not in the least lend itself to lovemaking (now that her own desire had passed). She wondered also what role she would play in it.

"Do you remember," continued her instructor, "that you asked us how we acted with young boys? Very well! The excellent woman who, with the majesty that you have seen, is ruling over this clandestine meeting, also can provide some pretty young boys of whom we are going to request an assortment."

He said several words to the servant, who disappeared. She came back in a minute with the Chinese woman with the wrinkled face who did her bows. Gino spoke briefly. The old woman bowed again, then uttered a sharp cry. The ugly girl who had prepared the pipes hurried to her.

"The old lady only speaks Chinese. But a Chinese that no one understands," explained Gino. "She has called the other back to serve as interpreter."

"And what language are you speaking?"

"Siamese."

He addressed himself to their hostesses again. After several minutes, Gino reported:

"She answered my request by offering something else. This conforms to the rules of this nature."

"What does she offer?"

"Girls, of course. I gave her the appropriate remonstrances. Then she suggested showing us some films."

"Oh!" said Michele. "Why not?"

"We didn't come here for so little. She also proposed to offer us a living spectacle. Two girls making love in front of us. There's nothing about that that could interest you is there, Michele?"

She made a face that could be interpreted as they wished.

Gino began his negotiations again, then said:

"I told her that we would like boys from

about twelve to fifteen with slender tongues and firm buttocks.

Michele covered her breast. The old woman was staring at her. She spoke again in a tone which shocked the young girl. The servant translated and Gino replied with a single word.

"What did she say?" asked Michele.

"She wanted to know if the boys were for me or for you."

"And . . . what did you answer?"

"For both of us."

Michele had the feeling that the walls were turning a little. Could it be the opium already? No, Gino had said . . .

The old woman was chanting again. She seemed to be lamenting, multiplying her bows, and finally finished on a piercing note, raising her arms to the heavens.

"I'm afraid it's not going to work out," said Gino even before he heard the translation.

"It's true," he confirmed later. "That crazy woman is trying to pretend that she doesn't have any boys available tonight. She says some strangers have already been here and took them away. She probably just wants to be paid a little more."

He began the discussion again. New gesticulations of disappointment followed. Gino insisted. Finally he said:

"She refuses. We'll have to go elsewhere."

He spoke to Coleman for a long time.

"He insists on staying here," he told Michele. "He's certain that he'll be able to get what he wants. I doubt it, but it's his business. I propose that we leave him here and start walking again. What do you say?"

Michele couldn't have asked for more. The atmosphere of the place was beginning to weigh on her. Nevertheless, she experienced an unexpected pain, almost a kind of remorse at leaving Coleman. "I accepted him as an intruder and spent the night hating his presence! We barely spoke to each other and now that I feel all weak toward him he wants to stay here. I must be out of my mind."

But she was still glad to leave.

They passed by the skeletons with the wild eyes again.

"Don't these two appeal to you?" she asked sarcastically.

She hated Gino and his friend for their insistence on procuring men. Couldn't they be satisfied with her for one night? Or, if they really didn't like women, why did they pretend to be so interested in her? And that idiot, Felicia! How could she have used such poor judgment in turning her over to pederasts? When she saw her again, she'd make her swallow her braids!

"What does Coleman find so attractive about boys?" she attacked. "It isn't very nice of him to leave us like that."

She was going to add with sudden resentment that he hadn't seemed so disgusted with girls when he was caressing her legs, but Gino didn't allow her time.

"The love of boys will always have a quality for men's tastes that that of women only possesses by exception," he said. "That is the quality of being abnormal. In other words, it satisfies the definition of the work of art as I told you earlier. Making love with a boy is to me erotic to the degree that it is against nature."

"Are you certain that it isn't quite simply in your nature?"

"I'm certain," said Gino. "I love women. Sex with a man has always been difficult for me to conceive of. I reasoned with myself and tried it last year for the first time. It's unnecessary to add that I was pleased with myself. You see that, even for me, it took a long time to develop my eroticism."

Michele was suffering from contradictory emotions. She wondered in particular what she should believe about Gino's allegations.

"And after that first experience, you practised your . . . art often?"

"I have always been careful to keep the rarety of things."

"But," insisted Michele, "have you also made love to women since then?"

Gino burst out laughing.

"What a question! Do I seem like a paragon of chastity to you?"

"A lot?" she wanted to know.

"Less, certainly, than I would have had if I had the luck to be a pretty woman."

He added, with a smile of homage for his companion:

"Men—and women lovers!"

This response did not satisfy Michele.

"Which do you like better?" she asked almost angrily.

Gino stopped. They had arrived at the spot where the clearing was replaced by the bridge. He took Michele by the shoulders and drew her to him. She thought he was going to kiss her.

"I love what is beautiful!" he said intensely. "And what is beautiful is never something already done and never something easy. It is what you make of life for the first time with your own movement and that of someone else, and it is what you throw to infinity before it had time to take its dead form."

'The man and the woman—another world in the middle of the created world.'

"What is beautiful is what didn't exist before you and wouldn't have existed without you and will no longer be in your power when the injustice of death has beaten you to this earth that you loved."

'Proud of their solitary knowledge, their exemplary plans.'

"What is beautiful is the moment that was nothing and which you have made unforgettable. It is the person who was nothing and whose singular mould you have erected against the amorphous multitude and destiny."

'Lost souls, throwing away the map of ready-made roads.'

"What is beautiful is to overcome your affection for your nation and your century, the fear of their scandal and of your disrepute, so that a new race can be born of your refusal to resemble your cowardly fathers, your faceless mothers, your hypocritical brothers, and your flabby sisters."

'Different—but of what ugliness?'

'Gone astray—but of what stupidity?'

'Foreigners—but to what herd?'

'Beaten—but for what revenge!'

'Exiled—but toward what future!'

"What is beautiful, is to hasten to discover,

to take your pleasures without weighing the dangers and without remembering past tenderness, it is to do what you have never tried before and what you will never experience again, because the days and nights of your life will only be those which you have enriched by an extraordinary act. And who, in heaven or on earth, will return the days and nights that you will have lost?"

'The moonlight petrifies them: the statue of Gino holds a woman's face in his hands.'

"What is beautiful is to try everything and refuse nothing, to be capable of knowing everything. Innumerable bodies that resemble us, men or women, Heaven or Hell, what difference is there . . ."

'On the four corners of the crossroad, empty straight, unreal, all similar bridges.'

"What is beautiful is he who never has the same taste, and who doesn't have a taste for anything else."

'The black hair on her naked shoulders between his fingers.'

"What is beautiful is to be the opposite of the gregarious, lazy, and shocking animal that one was born."

'The Tartar hero's shoulders hide the moon.'

"What is beautiful is not to stop yourself, not to sit down or go to sleep, and not to turn back."

'The night hours have turned, the steel stars gravitate out of sight in the lighted sky.'

"What is beautiful is to say no to the temptation which immobilizes you, which ties you down or limits you. And to say yes, always yes —no matter how tired you are, to whoever multiplies you and pushes you forward and forces you to do more than is sufficient or necessary and more than others would be content to do."

'The door half-opens on the yellow light. Shadows enter, shadows go out. Sleepless night.'

"What is beautiful, is to find a subject of new astonishment every day, a reason to be amazed, a pretext of effort and of victory over the temptation of acquisition and over the sadness and satiation of the age."

'My heart opens to your voice . . .'

"What is beautiful is to change untiringly. Because every change is progress, every permanence a tomb. Contentment and resignation are one in the same with despair, and he who stops and renounces becoming something else has already opted for death."

'The temple gong which is muffled by the noise of the insects.'

"Certainly at every moment it is your perfect right to prefer the peace of steles, to embalm yourself in the mediocrity of an existence without desires like a wax virgin in her jeweled shrine."

'Two children surge out of the shadows and pass, hand in hand.'

"But I who am trying to attract you not to death but to life, I say that it would have been better if you had not been born. Because each human life is a dead weight on our planet and the march forward of our species is curbed by it."

'They are brother and sister. They are going to make love.'

"Know this, Michele: the next days on this

earth will be what your body's power of invention will create. If your dream happens to be obscured and your wings close, if misfortune desires that your curiosity become fatigued, that your clairvoyance and your perseverance and your will to discover and renew give way—that is what makes the hopes and fortunes of men—the future will be eternally like the past."

'The white ballerina between the warrior's legs.'

"The love of loving is what makes you the world's fiancée. The destiny of everyone depends on your passion and your courage and if you renounce conquering a single man or woman it would be enough for the race to renounce conquering the lightyears and the nebulas."

'Gino's voice quiets the chant of the crickets.'

"Do you understand? It's not the pleasure of the moment that I bring you, but a much greater pleasure. Happiness is not at the place where you are, it is what you dream of attaining."

'Embraced by ever more numerous arms.'

"Oh yes, Michele! It is not illusions that I give you, but reality!" I am not teaching you the most convenient way. I am teaching you the most reckless way."

* * *

Michele said:

"Take me. You do not know me yet. I will have a new savor for you."

She was surprised to find so much respect in Gino's eyes. He shook his head.

"That would be too easy. I prefer this: let me lead you."

He pushed her in front of him.

She obediently walked ahead of him. When they reached the crossroad, Gino decided that they would take another path than the one that had brought them there.

"I'm going to show you something out of the ordinary," he promised.

They soon reached the edge of a large 'khlong'—or was it a natural river? It seemed to curve. Its banks were covered with herbs.

"Are we still in Bangkok?"

"Yes, but this place is not known by strangers."

They were walking in a prairie now and as Michele's heels were sinking into the ground, she removed her shoes.

"You're going to tear your stockings," said Gino. "Wouldn't you prefer to take them off?"

She was sensitive to this attention. She sat down on a broken tree trunk. She lifted her skirt. The fresh air made her remember that her panties were in Gino's pocket. The brightness of the moon was so intense that her abdomen was clearly visible as she undid her garterbelt.

"I never tire of the beauty of your legs," said Gino. "Your long thighs . . ."

"I thought that everything left you quickly?"

He smiled. She had no desire to move.

"Why don't you take your skirt off too?" he suggested. "It would be easier for you to walk that way. And it would please me to see you like that."

She didn't hesitate a second. She stood up and undid the belt.

"What am I going to do with it?" she asked,

holding the skirt out.

"Leave it on the tree. We'll get it on our way back. We have to pass by here anyway."

"What if someone steals it?"

"What difference does it make? I don't suppose you have any objection to going home without it, do you?"

Michele did not argue. They began walking again. Her buttocks and her legs appeared strangely pale under her black silk shirt. Gino was beside her. He took her hand.

"Here we are," he said in a few minutes.

A low wall, half collapsed, appeared before them. Gino helped his companion climb over the bricks and jump to the other side. When she lifted her head, she shuddered. A human form was crouching near them. Michele clutched Gino's hand.

"Don't be afraid. They're peaceful people."

She wanted to say: but his costume! Once again, the fear of Gino's sarcasm held her back. But she was so ashamed that she felt incapable of taking a step. She would have been less disturbed if she had been completely naked. Gino led her on inexorably. They passed the man who looked at them with burning eyes. Michele could not prevent herself from shivering.

"Look," said Gino, pointing his finger. "Have you ever seen anything like it?"

She followed the direction of his gesture. Strange fruits were hanging from a tree with an enormous trunk, veined with innumerable roots and adventitious liana. When she looked more carefully, Michele saw that they were phallus'. She let out a rather admiring exclamation. Gino explained:

"Some of them are votive offerings; others are offerings in order to obtain sexual potency or fecundity. Their size is a function of the wealth of the follower— or the urgency of his prayer. As you see, we are in a temple."

The thought made Michele remember the indecency of her attire.

"What if a priest found me like this . . ."

"You don't seem out of place here in a sanctuary dedicated to Priapus," said Gino, laughing. "Everything that is connected with his cult is permitted in this place."

"Is that what is called lingam?" asked Michele, whose curiosity was greater than her confusion.

"Not exactly. The lingam is Hindu, its design is generally stylized. You find it especially in the form of pillars tied vertically to the earth and most of the time it's impossible to identify what it is. Here, as you can see, the object's shape leaves nothing to the imagination. They are replicas of nature rather than works of art."

The cocks hanging from the branches ran from the size of a banana to that of a bazooka, but the realism of the details was the same in every case. They were all made of sculptured and colored wood. A little flesh-colored spot adorned the stem. The foreskin was represented by deep folds in the grain. The erect member's curvature was rendered with an impressive vitality.

There were hundreds of them hanging from several trees. Wax candles were placed here and there on the wood chandeliers. Most of them were extinguished but numerous incense burners identical to those that are lit before Buddha or on the ancestral altar and whose heady odor never leaves you, were burning in the garden. The incense that was being consumed pierced the night with its rosy tips.

Michele noticed with anguish that several of the candle-ends were moving. It didn't take a great effort to distinguish that human hands were holding them. It was not just one, but four, five, six, ten men at least. They were sitting on their heels like the first man they had met. One of them got up. She saw him approaching. When he was a few feet away, he kneeled down again. His face expressed a sustained and tranquil interest. Almost immediately two, then four, others joined him and stood beside him. One of the new ones appeared very young, almost a child. The others were older. One of them was almost an old man. No one said a word. They continued to hold the odoriferous rods between their joined fingers.

"There's a nice flowerbed," joked Gino. "What are we going to do with them?"

He pulled down one of the cocks with relatively modest proportions.

"I don't know whether I'm committing a sacrilege," he said, "but I'm doing it boldly. In any case, they don't seem to be offended."

He held the piece of wood out to Michele. "Isn't it pleasant to touch it?"

She felt it.

"Show them on this how you would use your hands if it were alive."

Michele obeyed without protesting and even with a certain relief, because for a moment she had been afraid that Gino would ask her to introduce the object into her body. The idea of its roughness and filthiness was revolting to her.

She caressed the article of devotion as if she really wanted to make it come. She began to believe in the parody herself. Soon she even practically regretted not being able to use her lips. But really, the instrument was too dusty!

She was conscious of the men's eyes on her. Their faces seemed peaceful. Gino made a movement. Almost immediately, she saw his cock standing up, bigger and redder than the wood penis.

"Now it's time for the illusion to give way to reality," said Gino. "Your hands must be as tender to flesh as they have been to an inanimate object."

Michele placed the object on a branch (she hadn't dared let it fall on the ground) and obediently seized Gino's cock. He turned so that the kneeling men could see better.

Time stopped. There wasn't the slightest sound. Michele remembered the 'humanism' whose principles Gino had recited earlier and she was trying so hard to follow them that she was dizzy. She no longer knew whether the pulsations in her hand were those of Gino or those of her own heart. She recalled his precept of making things last. Finally he murmured:

"Go on!"

At the same time, he turned toward the tree from which the priapic fruits were hanging. A flood of uncommon length and density flew from his cock through the night, sprinkling the wood cocks which were oscillating under the shock and pivoting at the end of their lines.

mouth, so far that her lips were touching the naked abdomen and her nose was buried in the sparse down. She remained like that a moment then, artfully, without trying to cheat or abridge, she began the coming and going motion in her mouth.

The experience, however, was a supplication to her and during the first moment of her fellation, she had to struggle against the nausea that was rising in her throat. It wasn't that she found the fact of giving herself to the love gestures with a young unknown boy degrading. The same game, if Gino had pushed her to it with a smart fair-haired child, smelling of cologne in the parlor of a Parisian friend would even have pleased her very much. Moreover, it was far from being the first time she had been unfaithful to her husband (without having the impression of deceiving him because with a child it would have sounded funny). Before leaving Paris she had given in to the advances of one of her own lover's baby brothers! They had been stopped a minute too late. Michele's consentment had already been acquired, not only in her mind, but very physically . . . The occasion had not offered itself again. She thought about it at this moment and thought that, everything considered, she was shameless by nature. That little boy who had known her humid cunt and had started to enter her! She had fucked ten times in her imagination since then. But with this one it wasn't the same thing. He didn't excite her at all. On the contrary, he frightened her. Besides she had been repulsed at first at the thought that he couldn't be clean. Fortunately, she felt reassured now and remembered with relief the meticulous ablutions which the Siamese practised several times a day. Nevertheless, this experience gave her no pleasure at all. She gave herself to it out of complaisance to Gino, but her senses and her tastes were repulsed . . .

Well, at least she ought to make a good job of it, she thought almost violently. A sort of pride urged her to treat this boy in a way that would leave him an ineffable memory. Hadn't her husband said that no woman in the world knew how to use their mouth for love the way she did?

Gradually she let herself be taken over by her own work, forgetting to whom the penis belonged and beginning to love its strength and warmth and letting the gland forage in her throat, searching for a place to finish its orgasm. She felt her lips and her clitoris becoming sensitive. She closed her eyes and let the sensations come over her. When her caresses attained their goal, the flow of sperm on her tongue gave her the same pleasure that it would have if it had been David's. The taste was different. She liked it. What difference did it make if all those men were watching her? She wanted to come in turn. Before the cock had withdrawn from her mouth, she touched the bud of her cunt and abandoned herself to an orgasm in Gino's arms as he kissed her lips for the first time.

"Didn't I promise to give you in detail?" he said after they had gone back over the wall. "Are you happy?"

She was. But she wasn't freed from her misery. She remained silent. He said dreamily:

"It is very important for a woman to drink a lot of sperm and from the most diverse sources."

His voice suddenly became ardent.

"You *must* do all this, because you are beautiful."

"Isn't it possible to be pretty and to remain good?" she sighed.

"You can certainly but at your own expense. Is it pardonable not to utilize the power of your beauty to obtain what so many graceless women cry out for in their dreams all their lives?"

"You seem to think that all women only dream of sex."

"Is there anything better?"

No one had stolen her skirt. She put it on and missed her preceding comfort. They took a new direction again which was different from the one she knew. She wondered if they were going to walk for much longer. When she was about to complain, they came out on a real street.

"We'll take a 'sam-lo,' if we can find one," said Gino.

Michele had never utilized this means of transportation, which had become rare, and the idea of trying it pleased her. It was more tempting to let oneself ride in the indolent rhythm of a pushcart under the bright moonlight than to risk death at each corner in a taxi. They walked along the street for a while before meeting a free vehicle. The driver (who was also called a 'sam-lo'), was sitting on the ground meditating. As soon as he saw them he motioned invitingly to the narrow bench covered with red velvet.

Gino chatted for a moment, probably discussing the price of the trip, then signaled for Michele to get in. He sat down next to her. Although they were both remarkably slender, they were crushed against one another. Gino put his arm around her shoulders and she pressed against him happily. When she sat down she had raised her skirt very high since he had said that he liked her legs. The tricycle shook. Suddenly she had an idea which seemed fantastic and wild even to her. She had never done such a thing on her own and what's more, in the street! But she was going to do it. She gathered all her courage.

She turned a little on her side toward Gino. With one hand she undid his buttons. Then she hastily lowered the zipper. She slid her hand in and took the sleeping cock between her fingers. Then she sighed deeply.

"That's good, Michele!" said Gino. "I'm very proud of you."

"Really?"

"Yes. Your actions were right because the custom is for the man to take the initiative and the woman to be submissive. A woman who takes the initiative when the man least expects it creates the most worthy erotic situation. Bravo!"

She felt in her hand that Gino's approbation was not purely spiritual.

"Remember that formula in other circumstances," he continued, "and you'll do well." It goes without saying that she remained submissive to the clause of novelty according to the rule.

"How's this?" she asked.

She began to caress Gino gently.

"If you were the mistress of a gentleman and you removed your clothes in front of him even without him asking you first, where is the unexpected? And also, where is the eroticism? But if your ambassador at breakfast time has introduced you to a visiting diplomat so that you could show him the temple of Buddha and you have invited him to have tea in your little parlor, ah, well, then. You alleviate the fatigues of this tour of the city! You seat yourself beside him on your best white silk sofa, and quite simply remove your blouse, shaking your hair naturally.

"This spontaneous gesture would leave an imperishable mark in your guest's memory. On his death bed, it would be your face that would come to haunt him and console him. After this debut naturally a whole gamut of possibilities is at your disposal. You may temporarily limit your initiate and with your breasts naked, ceremoniously pour his tea without forgetting to ask him whether he ordinarily takes one or two lumps of sugar. There is a strong chance that at the moment he will be incapable of remembering. Moreover, it is from this that you can recognize what action is the most appropriate. If he is troubled to the point of saying eight or fourteen or a foot, don't wait for him to make the next move. Decide on two lumps and move closer. Operate as you just did with me and ask him what he prefers: to come before or after drinking his tea and in what way—in your hand, in your mouth, or in your cunt. From this moment on, the rest is of little importance. The climate has been created. And the work of art, as you like to call it, is on its way. If, on the contrary, your visitor has conserved a semblance of self-control, let him do what he wants himself, that is to say throw himself on you and act like the animal you have unleashed in him, and you will only benefit from it. If you wish to vary it, you will remove not only your blouse, but everything, without for a moment ceasing to be the woman of the world and without manifesting the slightest emotion. When, holding your skirt in your left hand, you have skipped over the circle with your long dancer's legs and have let yourself fall back on a pillow, when you have taken off your panties and put them in a safe place in the vase of orchids, you will sit down again on your traveler's left and lean back gently on the cushions with a friendly smile. If your guest seems paralyzed with surprise, put him at his ease by telling him how you were violated the night before by two blacks armed with machetes and how much pleasure you had. Describe in detail your tormentors' cocks and the liberties they took with your body. If he still doesn't move, masturbate in front of him. Finally, for the third experience, with another guest, don't undress at all but, after having lifted the teapot and before asking him about the sugar, you will ask very simply: 'After we have had tea, would you like to make love? My husband will not be back before one o'clock.' If by chance the individual tries to hide, on the pretext of an old wound, a vow pronounced at the bedside of his Carmelite godmother, or a disposition for the Code of Hammurabi forbidding him to come before sundown, you will say in a clear tone of voice and without manifesting any anger: 'You are right: what was I thinking? I also promised to be faithful when I was married and since I have never deceived my husband, it would be better that I not start today.' The imbecile will never be able to console himself for having let the rare pearl that you are escape. If he changes his mind, be unapproachable from then on. Let him try to abuse your innocence and you call the police and have him condemned. No jury will have any faith in the allegations he advances in his defense—the truth!"

Michele was enchanted by the dimension which Gino's member had taken because of her work. She told him so without trying to hide her sarcasm.

"Dear professor, the words that you suggest I utter are exactly those, if memory serves me, that I addressed you with less than an hour ago. Since you have injuriously repulsed me, I'm going to turn you over to the first policeman who passes us."

Gino smiled.

"I love your hand," he said. "Don't move it. My dear, don't try to pass for more stupid than you are. You know very well that there is no connection between the situation that I was describing and our relationship."

Michele did not completely see where the difference was unless it was in the absence of the tea. Nevertheless, she was in no mood or state to argue. The caresses she was giving were inflaming her own senses. Even the bumps of the tricycle on the rough ground added to her pleasure.

"That 'sam-lo' doesn't know the spectacle he's missing," remarked Gino.

He whistled. The man immediately turned his head. His eyes leaped from one to the other passenger, lighting his face with a huge smile.

"We're making him happy," remarked Michele.

"Yes, we have found an accomplice," said Gino. "There's nothing surprising about that, because it's beautiful. There's an international appreciation for beauty. A certain number of things are only permitted to those who are beautiful. Montherlant, writing to Pierre Brasseur, remarked one day that 'Indecency is not at all vulgarity. It's prudishness that is vulgarity.' "

"Courteline said before him, "cited Michele, very proud of her knowledge, " 'the true modesty consists in hiding what is not beautiful."

"Are you ashamed of your breasts, then?"

"Oh, no!"

With her free hand, she pulled her sweater out of her skirt and tried to push it over her head. Gino helped her. For a moment she had to leave his stiff prick, but it was only for a brief interlude.

"Now I would like someone to see us," said Gino.

"Isn't the 'sam-lo' enough as a witness?" pleaded Michele in spite of herself.

"He's no longer a witness, he's part of it."

Gino called him again and the Siamese man turned around on his saddle. He seemed extremely impressed by the quasi-nudity of his passenger and the tricycle lurched. They all laughed loudly. Michele had the impression that she was a little intoxicated. It was too late for it to be the effects of the Chianti.

Gino's wish was granted. A car passed them and Michele thought it was going to stop. Her heart was pounding. The car took off again, however. It had been impossible to distinguish the faces of the occupants.

"Perhaps it was one of your friends?" suggested Gino cruelly.

She did not reply. She preferred to think only of caressing him. Another 'sam-lo,' carrying two American marines, was passing them. They let out great cries when they discovered the spectacle. Gino and Michele pretended neither to see or hear them. The others motioned desperately, trying to make the two vehicles stop, but their drivers did not falter, continuing to press on the pedals in a regular rhythm.

"Where would you prefer to come?" asked Michele. "In my hand, in my mouth, or in my cunt?"

He did not reply immediately. She leaned over and took him in her lips, pushing his cock deep into her mouth.

Before he had time to answer her question, they found themselves in front of the gate of Gino's garden.

He leaped out of the tricycle, escaping his companion's hands, and readjusted his clothing. Michele stepped down but did not judge it necessary to put her pullover on again which was dangling over her arm with her purse. Her breasts had an admirable shape under the moonlight.

Gino opened the gate. The 'sam-lo' had

stepped down and was waiting without any visible emotion, apparently for his payment. The Italian leaped onto the saddle so quickly that the man didn't have time to do anything. His vehicle was already in the garden with Gino pedaling at top speed. The Siamese man and Michele remained facing one another. They both burst out laughing at the same time. The young man was taking his client's jest in his stride. For the moment he seemed more preoccupied with admiring Michele's figure than with retrieving his property. It was she who set out in pursuit of the fugitive first. She found him in front of the perron of tree trunks. He was standing and holding the vehicle by the handlebar.

"You're so crazy!" the young woman reprimanded tenderly.

"I like your breasts too," he announced.

"I'm so lucky!" she answered sardonically.

She was more flattered than she wanted to admit. The 'sam-lo' joined them, still laughing. Gino spoke to him. It was a veritable speech with intonations, silences, and great eloquence. Michele wondered what he could be saying. The man's face did not reflect anything which permitted any hypotheses. Suddenly he answered, looking at Michele at the same time. Gino began his speech again. The boy shook his head affirmatively.

"It's all settled and I've found my man!" said Gino. "It's funny how you can search everywhere for what is waiting for you at your own door!"

"What? You mean . . ."

"Yes! Don't you think he's worthy of my favors?"

This time Michele felt almost on the verge of tears. Gino's niceties during their ride had made her forget his earlier repulses. She was more or less consciously waiting for him to take her in his arms once they were in the house. She was ready to spend the rest of the night there if he desired it and not even thinking of going home. He could have done whatever he wanted with her. And now it turned out that he didn't want anything. The only thing he had on his mind was finding a boy for his bed! Michele turned her tear-stained face toward the boy. She couldn't see him distinctly. Was he really so beautiful then? She remembered having thought he had the look of a boxer . . .

"Cara! Don't start tormenting yourself in advance again," said Gino gaily, interrupting as usual Michele's somber reflections. "You'll see, I have a wonderful idea. Come in quickly."

He opened the door and pulled her in, holding her by the waist. She allowed him to lead her without ceasing to pout. She had enough ideas about Gino. She was happy all the same to be back in the room with its zones of shadows and light, the red leather couch, and the odor of the 'khlong.' It didn't seem that many boats were passing by. It was too late—or too early. She suddenly felt sleepy. What a night!

Gino brought some enormous glasses which contained a green liqueur.

"Here's something that will revive my beloved!"

His beloved? Michele smiled bitterly. The

'sam-lo' was standing in the middle of the room and seemed a little embarrassed. He took the drink Gino held out to him with obvious nervousness. All three drank in silence. She was so thirsty that she emptied her glass in one gulp. Gino was right. She felt revived. He sat down quickly next to her and put his arms around her. He placed his lips on her left breast.

"I'm going to take you," he cried.

He waited to judge the effect of his words.

Michele was too stunned to show anything. Besides, she wasn't convinced.

"But I'm going to take you through this handsome shepherd," continued Gino. "Through, in the proper meaning of the word. That is to say that I'm going to go through him to reach you. I'm going to possess you as you have never been possessed and as I have never possessed a woman. You will be more mine than any other being has ever belonged to another. Do you consent?"

Michele did not understand what he was trying to say—or she refused to understand. But whatever he was asking, it was good and she accepted it. The only thing that she had feared was that he would not ask anything. She said:

"Do anything you want to me."

For the second time, he kissed her on the lips. Now she was completely happy, and impatient for him to take her.

"Your first lover!" he cried. "You're going to have him tonight."

She was ashamed of herself for having lied to him, for not having admitted her adventures on the plane to Gino. But was it important? In a sense, because it was the first time that she was giving her complete consent, in complete lucidness and in complete recognition. She wanted to be an adulteress, and he would really be her first lover.

"The first of many others?" he asked as if to assure himself that she had assimilated her lesson.

"Yes," said Michele.

How wonderful it was to abandon herself so completely! The woman who gives herself to one person cannot know what steps the woman is taking who promises herself completely to many, to an unlimited number of men. No woman ever would be as adulterant as she was at this moment. Who else could achieve the miracle of deceiving her husband for the first time, deceiving him with all those who would want her from now on?

"You will never refuse?" insisted Gino.

She shook her head. She was thinking: if he orders me to give myself to ten men tonight, I'll do it.

He only asked her to give herself to the 'sam-lo.' She took off her skirt and stretched out on the couch, leaning on the thick cushions whose softness enchanted her. She held her legs apart, her heels resting on the floor, and she put her arms around the man's buttocks when he began to introduce himself carefully in her. When he was completely in, Gino, who had remained beside Michele until then, holding her, got up and went to place himself behind the 'sam-lo.' He seized the boy's flanks and Michele felt his hands touching hers.

She heard the moans of pleasure escaping his lips. At certain moments they were almost cries.

"Now, I am in you," said Gino. "I'm piercing you with a sword two times more sharp than that of ordinary men. Do you feel it?"

"Yes. I'm happy," said Michele.

The Siamese boy's hard penis withdrew from her body and came back inexorably, beginning his path again and again and accelerating gradually. She did not try to find out if Gino would permit her to come: she screamed immediately. Her body convulsed on the satiny leather. The two men joined their moans to hers. Their confused cry tore the night and some dogs in the distance responded with an interminable concert of barks. But the trio paid no attention to them. They existed in another world. An interior harmony seemed to reign over them like the wheels of a watch. They had succeeded in constituting a profound unity without fissures, more perfect than even a couple can form. The Siamese boy's hands pressed Michele's breasts and she was sobbing with pleasure, arching her back so that he could enter her farther, panting that she was happier than she could stand and begging him to tear her—not to spare her and to come in her.

Gino felt that the 'sam-lo's' strength was inexhaustible, but he couldn't go on. He dug his nails into his partner's flesh as if for a signal. The two men ejaculated simultaneously, the 'sam-lo' deep in Michele's body, swooning under another thrust. Michele cried even harder than she had cried up to then, feeling the bitter taste of semen which was inundating her rise in her throat. Her voice ricocheted on the black water, without anyone being able to tell to whom the cry was addressed:

"I love you! I love you! love you!"